BEAUTIFULLY BUILT

Built For You Book 1

TH Compton

May you remember you are beautiful and sexy no matter how you are built.

CONTENTS

1

LOGAN

Waking up is hard, especially when the first thing you see when you open your eyes is cat ass. Hulk jumped off my chest as I rolled over to turn off the alarm clock. The kitten glared at me with her fiery green eyes and ran towards the kitchen, probably to wait for me by her bowl. I sat up, groaning and body cracking as I stretched. *God, isn't twenty-five too young for my body to make this much noise when I move?* At least it was Friday and I would have the weekend to sleep in and do as little as possible.

As predicted, Hulk was mewing by her bowl as soon as I stepped foot in the kitchen. I wished more than ever that I never started giving her wet food because that fishy stench was a lot to face first thing in the morning, but she was used to it now and would throw a kitty fit if I tried to give her dry food. "You are such a spoiled brat," I said as I hissed at her. The only response I received was a small yowl as she rubbed her body against my legs. "You are lucky that you are cute and cuddly. Now be good while I get ready." I knew there was a fifty-fifty chance I would come home to a mess of something being knocked over or cabinets riffled through, but I was running late so it would have to wait.

Clean and dressed in a gray vest and button up combo, I was once again faced with the mirror and not liking what I saw. Some days I kinder to myself, but feeling stuffed into my jeans for casual Friday never inspired self esteem. I know I am chunky, hefty, big boned or whatever other way it can be said; some days I just embraced it, but today was not one of those days. At five foot seven inches, I'm short and chubby. I can't abide the word fat. I mean, I know it's true, but if I have to label myself then I'd rather be a chubby twink. I just needed to get to work so I could focus on something else. Hopefully checking off my to-do list and playing with numbers would improve my mood.

It didn't. In fact, I felt even more out of sorts. Being the office manager at Tolson Accounting Firm meant I wore many hats and was sort of the office B and add an itch, for lack of a better term. Honestly, I enjoyed it most days, because I was never bored and I like solving peoples' problems. Today there were just too many, and by lunch I had a mountain of projects to handle as well as orders to place. I would add them to my list and chip away at it once my break was done. I walked over to Java Script, the local coffee shop, to grab a pesto chicken sandwich and an iced tea to see me through the day when my best friend, Syl, texted me.

Syl: When are you gonna be home?

Logan: I will probably be a little late finishing up some things so I don't dread Monday all weekend. Why what's up?

Syl: Mondays suck regardless. Get home soon so you can save me from your cat.

Logan: That key was for emergencies and I thought you had to work today?

Syl: I did early morning inventory so I got to leave after. Anyway I am napping on your couch so we can hang tonight.

Logan: It's already been a long day and I am so ready for the weekend. Netflix and chill tonight? I am placing you in charge of the pizza, but I am begging you for the millionth time NO GREEN PEPPERS on my half.

To this I got no reply. I figured he and Hulk were already passed out napping on my couch with reruns of Law and Order in the background. His crush on Benjamin Bratt had taken on a life of its own. The only other reason I could think of for Syl not being glued to his phone was that he was neck deep in some sort of new lotion or treatment from the store he works at. Having an esthetician as a best friend has its perks, but it also means that everytime he comes over somehow every surface ends up sticky with product. I grabbed my lunch and headed back to work so I could put in some work orders while I munched.

The rest of the day went pretty smooth. The phone wasn't ringing off the hook, so I got a lot more accomplished than I thought I would by five o'clock. I even got compliments on how many leads I gathered for the team, and my boss, Mr. Richardson, gave me some new responsibilities to tackle next week to see if I could handle some of the marketing for the company. I shut down my computer for the day feeling satisfied if not a little brain fried from the earlier stress. I was so looking forward to a nice night in with pizza and maybe some hard cherry seltzer. Hopefully, I could talk Syl into letting me pick the movie.

2

CAINE

I was gearing up for another busy Friday night at the bar. Emmett, co-owner of Built Bar and my ride or die best friend, was going over the list of upcoming events we needed to start promotions on at his place. He lived above our bar, so that says all that needs to be said about his work life balance. I was the face of our partnership, handling most of the staffing and front of house work, and he stayed behind the scenes, running our social media and books. We have been good friends since we met working at a rooftop beach bar and restaurant in our early twenties. After that, we job hopped around together over the years from bar to bar until we decided to go into business together. So we've had a good working track record.

"Built Bar is turning more into a nightclub with the added performers and music we play. We'll have to hire more security, and maybe even consider trying to expand in the future to make a bigger dance floor." I told Em as he shot me a dirty look. "Stop fucking scowling at me. Business is great! This is a good thing."

"I'm not scowling at you and you know it--asshole." Em said, the paralyzed portion of his face frozen and the left side in a frown. Emmett suffered from a severe case of Bell's Palsy a few years back, and it permanently damaged the nerves in the right side of his face and darkened his outlook on just about everything.

I stared right at him, "You know I can tell your facial expressions, and I can tell you were scowling at that idea. I don't even notice your face. I know it's a big deal to you, but I never notice the paralysis unless you mention it. So what don't you like about expanding? We've been in the bar business for seven years now and have weathered everything together just fine."

"I just never wanted to have such a big club crowd. I know it's good, but it's getting to be a lot to manage. You've been taking on more shifts in the bar as it is." Em looked frustrated and I could tell he felt guilty that he didn't want to be out in the bar more.

"True, I have been. I might need your help on the floor from time to time, but we're doing okay." I reached my hand out to his and held it for a moment to reassure him. I knew he didn't want to face having to be out in public more even if I think it would be good for him.

"Hah, I am not going out there on display. You can be the pretty boy mixing drinks and getting numbers. I'll stick with the back office." He said, shaking his head.

"You know you can't hide forever. Besides, this business is your baby. I just wanted to help run a bar and took the leap with you. I know you miss being out there."

"I'm just not ready. Not yet. Let's get through the month, and if these events go well we can talk again about expanding."

"Fine, but I want to see some baby steps. Help me with some of the upcoming interviews for some more bouncers and bartenders. We'll need to get more hired and trained with Nathan leaving and Marta going down to part time for school."

He rolled his eyes at me, but I knew I'd gotten my way. "I'll start advertising the positions online and see about getting something set up."

I gathered up my notes and headed downstairs to check that we were ready to open. Kelly, our bar manager, greeted me with a sarcastic smile. "It's about time, boss. You better have a good excuse for leaving me shorthanded for prep. I hope you weren't getting laid in the back." Sometimes Kelly could come on a little strong personality-wise, but she meant well. I know she would fight for me, but I also know she will tell me about myself bluntly –*very* bluntly.

"Geez Kelly, I was with Emmett. I wouldn't leave you hanging over a fucking hookup."

"Good, because you're getting too old to be a hooking up with a new guy every night. How's Emmett? It's been a while since he's left that apartment, and I'm getting a little worried. I don't suppose he'll grace us with his presence tonight? You know Russ called out."

"You know I can fire you, right? Like, I am in charge." I gave her the side eye and tried my best to look stern because she was in a wiley mood this evening. She responded by laughing in my face. Man, I could tell she was going to poke at me all night, but I guess I did spend too much time shooting the shit upstairs once Em and I finished business when I should have been helping. "Shit Kell, I didn't know Russ wasn't going to show. Now I do feel bad that you're shorthanded. I'll stay behind the bar tonight with you. I'll call Chris and see if he'd be willing to pull a few extra hours to help us barback. Do you forgive me now?"

"I guess so. I know we can handle it now boss, but the weekends are getting a lot busier. Any word on new hires? Oh, and don't think

I didn't notice you sidestepping about Emmett." She was looking at me like she was my mother and caught me in a lie.

"Emmett is Emmett, and no he won't be joining us. I did talk him into doing some interviews with me down the line. He's not happy about it and is probably freaking out and cleaning his whole apartment now, but I think he knows it's time." I cut up fruit while we continued to chat and she threw jabs at me about how many numbers I'd get tonight. She wants me to be happy, but I won't settle for someone just to not be alone. And I refused to feel bad about sleeping around. I was safe and I enjoyed sex.

"You know you're getting old," She said yet again. "You should settle down with one of these guys before you lose your luster," she said with her chin held high and a big ass smile. "You already complain about your body aching and you're almost forty."

"I'm only thirty-five, and you are kind of the worst friend ever. My body hurts because I work too much and I need a new mattress. I'm not losing anything. I get better with age. Besides, I'm not going to date someone randomly just because."

She shook her head as she said, "All teasing aside Caine, you really should look for someone to be with for more than a night, someone special. Aren't you tired of hookups?

"Am I tired of sex?–Hell No–but I wouldn't mind someone special. None of these hookups have felt like anything more. Even the ones that were more than once just felt like fuckbuddies. Heck, some of them turned into actual friends, which is great, but there has been no spark apart from my dick being interested."

"Ugh, fine, I get it, but just keep a more open mind and tell your dick to cool it till you at least have dinner with them or something more than a trip to your apartment." I knew she was getting frustrated with me and I knew her heart was in the right place. She worried I would never take a break from the bar and give myself the chance to find more, but I can't help it. If it isn't more than sexual attraction, then I'm not going to force it. I cut up fruit and checked to see what inventory needed changing before we opened, and our conversation veered off into regular day to day work things.

We had a steady stream of patrons coming in for happy hour. I always enjoy the time before things get too crazy. It's nice to just shoot the shit with the regulars and get into the routine with my staff. Eventually I would have to mingle a bit more and talk up the next performer we were hosting, but honestly, I feel more at home behind the bar. It looked like it was shaping up to be a good night for the bar, and I was hoping I could find someone to unwind with a little later.

3

LOGAN

"Today was brutal," I said as I walked in my apartment.

"I know, right." Syl said as he was lounging on my couch flipping channels. "I just want to let loose for the weekend. Maybe find some hottie to plow me into the mattress."

Gosh, he probably just woke up from sleeping on my couch all afternoon and he still looks ready for a night on the town. "Have fun with that. I just want comfy pants, Paul Rudd, and pizza."

"Paul Rudd?"

"Yea, Ant Man." Syl looked at me clueless. "Paul Rudd plays Ant Man in the movies and in the Avengers." Syl just shrugged. "O. M. G. Paul Rudd. He's really funny but in the sarcastic dry way we like."

"Ok, well, unless he's coming over, has a sizeable cock, and is into threesomes, I don't care." Syl came over and grabbed my wrists, swinging them back and forth. "We are going out!"

"Nope, no way, not happening. One - today is one of those days where I feel like the giant Stay Puft Marshmallow Man." I whined as

I held up my finger. "Two - I know we had pizza and movie plans," holding up a second finger. "And three - you have never had a three-some, so don't make fun of my man."

"Come on, please, I really want to go out. Doesn't a drink with friends sound better than bug boy?" Syl fluttered his eyelashes and stared me down.

"Oh sure, I just bared my soul about how crappy I feel I look and how rough today was and you propose shoving me in a room full of people and loud music so I can feel even more awkward and ugly. Not to mention I know you too well and you'll want me to dance with you, which is the last thing I want to do."

"Hold up, we've been through this over and over. All that trash talk is in your head. No one thinks as badly about you as you do about yourself. Also yes, drinking with friends is generally a good way to cheer up and relax. So you get your ass in your room and put on that new sweater you got last time we went to the mall. You know, the black one with the embroidered feathers." Syl continued as he made his way through my apartment to my closet. "Throw that over ––something–." He threw the word out of his mouth like it was distasteful, looking bewildered at my clothing selection. "Good gracious Logan, I know I never see you in color, but you truly have nothing bright."

I looked at him blankly. "Um, how long have you known me? This isn't new." I started mentally thinking what jewelry I could pair with my outfit, trying to psych myself up to go out.

"We were practically in the womb together. I understand you feel the need to blend into the background, but god, Logan, the most vivid color you own is gray."

"I like gray," said Logan.

"Lo, I love you with all my heart ––every fiber of my being, but gray is like the most depressing color. It is the anti statement of intensity. It's dull and forgettable, two things you are not. Please consider going with me to get some colorful t-shirts at least. You can wear them under all the black and gray. I'll take it slow–I know it's your first time." He's playing it off like a joke, but he looked so sincere as he patted my chest and tried to tell it like it is. I knew he was trying to be sweet, and he had a point.

I gave in. "Fine, but if I say yes, can we postpone going out until I have a more Syl approved wardrobe?" I knew he won't let me wallow, but I just didn't want to deal with people right now.

"Nope, and Samuel and Devon are already waiting for us." He said in an innocent voice.

I turned on him, gobsmacked as his words sank in. "You mean to tell me this was all arranged, and you didn't tell me?"

"Lo, if I would have told you, you would have worked yourself up about it and thought of a million ways to weasel out of it."

He's not wrong. I would have had a list of reasons ready to bail out. I know I will have some fun once I go out, but the anticipation and actually working up the courage to do it always sends my head spinning.

"Now throw that on and let's feed your hell spawn it's dinner so we can go."

"Hulk is not a hell spawn. You two just got off on the wrong foot."

"Hah, ain't that the truth. One tends to form opinions of demon cats when they shit inside your Doc Martens," he said loudly enough for the cat to hear no matter where it is in the apartment.

"She was just a baby then and those dress shoes were old as dirt." I really didn't want him bad mouthing my baby. That was my job, and she can be really sweet... well, to me at least.

"You've only had her for like six months! Besides, those shoes were perfect and broken in to the point of peak comfort," he said as he was rooting through my underwear drawer. "Ah ha! Here is where all the color is. Yes to the hot pink boxer briefs for tonight! Sexy, sexy." He tossed them at me triumphantly.

"God, you're annoying," I said as I changed my clothes. Syl is the only person I would ever feel comfortable changing in front of. "You know I like bright colors and fashion. I just don't like it on me. I'll stick with my accessories. They're one size fits all."

"Shut up. There are plenty of stylish clothes that would fit you just fine and you'd rock the hell out of them. God, YOU are so annoying when you're having one of your mopey days. That's why I'm getting you out," he says as he tries to hurry me along.

I was finally dressed, and I looked in the mirror. *I don't look half bad,* I thought as I ran my fingers across the stitching of the feathers. I plucked a few chains out of my collection to wear around my neck. They were gunmetal but looked sort of like an oil slick with greens and pinks when it shifted in the light. It was the finishing touch and gave me an extra boost of confidence. I felt ready, or as ready as I was going to feel. "Let me feed her and let her know I'll be gone for a while then we can...Wait, where are we going?"

"That place they were telling us about down near the pier, Built Bar. Oh, and did you just say you have to tell your cat where you are going? Do you have to ask permission too? You really are becoming a crazy cat lady," he sighed.

"Oh, eat soap, Syl," I rebutted, "And isn't it bad enough that we live in vacation beach body central, but now they are actually naming bars after body types? They might as well have a sign that says no one over a forty inch waist may enter here. Stay out Logan."

Syl rolled his eyes and asked, "Are you done yet? Good because we both need a drink and a fuck if we can get it." I balked at him.

"I have had sex with four people in my whole life, all of which you have heard the tragic tales and helped me through the aftermath, and yet you think I want to pull tonight?"

He huffed, "The men you slept with never wanted relationships. You just hoped they would. I am sorry those assholes didn't want more from you, but it is completely their loss. However, if you make the choice going in it just wanting to get laid then wham bam thank you ma'am and you can just enjoy some fun."

"There is nothing fun about getting undressed in front of someone."

Syl froze and his smile faded. "Is that really how you feel Lo? I'm sorry, and I don't mean to tease and poke at you for wanting something more than sex. You are beautiful, and one day you'll find someone who will make you believe it."

"Nope, it'll just be me and Hulk and her nine furry siblings forever," I joked, but I knew Syl wouldn't laugh. "Listen, I heard you, I promise. I'm just not in the mood to be so serious anymore." I saw the concern in Syl's eyes and I felt bad for bringing him down. "Let's go out with the guys and have some fun. Woo!" I said, trying to lighten the tension that'd built.

"This conversation isn't over, but it's tabled for now," Syl said in a warning tone. Then in a total three-sixty, "Let's get our flirt on and Friday it up!"

I fed and pet Hulk on the head as she swatted at my hand, and then I followed Syl out the door, only slightly dreading the evening to come.

4

CAINE

The bar was slammed. I knew it would be, but without Russ, we really were hustling. I took a moment and grabbed a towel to wipe the sweat off my brow. I scanned the floor to make sure tables were being cleared and everyone was having a good time. The guest DJ we hired for the weekend was amazing, blasting beats that had the dance floor filled with all types of pretty people. It was cold for early February, but that didn't stop club goers from sweating and showing some skin. I liked how Built ran the line of local gay bar and hot night spot. No matter how much we decided to expand, I didn't want us to lose the fantastic charm we started with. I'm a local boy, and I wanted this to be for us and not just a tourist attraction for vacationers.

"Boss, we need five rum and cokes all day," Kelly shouted, knocking me out of my daydream. I signaled that I've got her back and started on the set when I heard the most unusual laugh. It was an effervescent giggle, like the bubbles from my soda gun. I couldn't believe how funny something had to be for a laugh to be heard over this music.

I went through the motions of making drinks while I searched for the owner of the bubbly laughter. Finally, I spotted a table of men in the back corner, where a short blond man was covering his face trying to contain his laughter. I kept watching as he wiped tears of joy from his eyes. I finally got a look at his face, and his pale skin was stunning under the pink lights flashing in time to the music. His friend—or maybe boyfriend— stood up and dragged him onto the dance floor as the beat shifted. I felt nauseous at the idea that he might already be taken.

I tried to focus on filling orders, but my eyes kept going back to bubbles trying to take in more details about him. He was stocky, but it fit him. I liked his fuller figure. He had sort of an apple shape, and I watched his sweet ass sway to the music. He was a decent dancer and just having fun. It was odd to me that he danced with his eyes closed and he couldn't stay in one spot. I don't know how he wasn't running into the other people. He had a clunky sort of grace about him, and I got the feeling he wanted to forget everything in the room but the music. The song ended and bubbles headed back to the table with his group. The man he was dancing with walked past the bar towards the restroom. I noticed he sparkled as he went by, probably from some sort of body glitter, and normally he would be just what I was looking for, but my eyes returned to my bubbly man.

I watched him interact with his friends with big hand gestures, his head whipping back and forth to include everyone in conversation. My mind wondered. I imagined how soft his skin would be and if he would be ticklish when I caressed him. Okay I did more than watch, I stared shamelessly at him as I worked hoping he would turn around so I could take in his beauty. I wanted him. Fuck yes I wanted him, but it was more than just wanting to take him to bed. I wanted to hear that laugh again. I wanted to be the one to make him laugh. I wanted to know him.

5

LOGAN

I hated to admit it, but I was having a good time. Syl was right, I felt more relaxed and less self conscious than I had been feeling. Devon broke through my musings when he interrupted the conversation. "Don't turn around, Logan, but that bartender has been eyefucking you since you went on the dance floor." I raised my eyebrows with a skeptical look and he continued. "I'm serious. You can't see him, but I can, and he wants a piece of you, babes. And that means you can go to the bar and get the next round," he said, winking at me.

"Oh no, no, no –I am not going up there," I said as I glanced at the man staring in our direction. He was the sexiest man of life, and there was no way he was interested in me. *Although he did look like he was watching me.* I quickly turned my head. "He must be looking at Syl. I mean, he literally shines tonight."

Syl glowed but then let me have it. "No way, that gorgeous ginger is totally about you right now. So suck it up, buttercup, and go order me my signature drink."

"Oh come on, Syl, no fair. No one wants to order you Pink Squirrels. Can't you pick something simple? Or try one of the specials like Devon and Samuel. You like your–." I paused as I scanned the table tent. "Your Built Blushtinis –right?" *I inwardly cringed as I felt unsure if I wanted to order those from the sexy barman either.*

"Yep, real good," Samuel and Devon said in unison, nodding.

"I like my Pink Squirrel. It's creamy and sweet. What's not to love?" Syl said suggestively. I rolled my eyes at him and looked to see that the bartender was still staring at me. I really didn't want to go, but I knew the guys wouldn't let it drop.

"This is going to be so embarrassing," I mumbled as the boys sent me on my way. I approached the edge of the bar and was relieved when the bartender's attention was focused elsewhere, taking someone else's order. I breathed deeply as the female bartender came my way. Just as she was about to ask me what I want, the man practically shoved her out of the way and told her he's got it, directing her to finish the shots he was pouring. She scowled at him but did what he said, and now he was face to face with me.

"What can I get you, sweetheart?" he said, and I swear I saw his eyes twinkle. I felt my face heat as I stared at his blinding smile. *He's just flirting for a tip. Pull yourself together and get this whole situation over with so you can go drink in the corner with your back to him.* "Uh...sweetie? What can I get you?" Sexy McBartender said.

Oh hell, words.... "Yeah, sorry – I need a gin and tonic, two martini specials, and a Pink Squirrel," I said as quickly and nonchalantly as possible so maybe he would just let the retro drink slide on by like people order them all the time.

He cocked his head, "A what now? Did you just say a Pink Squirrel?" I nodded, still trying to keep it cool even though I was turning as pink as the drink was supposed to be. "I don't think I have ever actually had anyone order that here. I think that's something my grandmother liked. I can make a more modern day version, but that's kind of obsolete."

"That's fine," I muttered as he started making the drinks in front of me with flair. He even tossed a bottle behind his back and caught it. It was––pretty impressive.

"So do you share other interests of fifties housewives?" The bartender said with a smirk as he made the Pink Squirrel.

"Hah, um, no; it is for my friend."

"The sparkly one, the one tall guy, or the one who is obviously watching us right now?" He chuckled and as he moved on to preparing my gin and tonic.

"That would be the sparkly one, but Syl only orders it because he thinks it's silly, so he has deemed it his signature cocktail."

"It is an interesting name."

"Yeah, but he just likes to make people order them for him and make jokes about how creamy they are...." I stopped, realizing what I just said to the absolute stranger. This extremely hot stranger. God, if I didn't already want to disappear, I definitely did now. A hole could have opened up in the floor and I would have gladly jumped into it. I grimaced and looked up at him through my lashes, and I could tell he was holding in his laughter.

"Your friend sounds like a funny guy. It's not everyday someone orders a drink to make cum innuendos." I was speechless. Did he really just say that? He's as brazen as Syl and Devon combined. He seemed confused when I didn't continue the conversation, so he went on. "This is probably too much for you to carry back yourself. I can watch the Pink Squirrel and the gin and tonic if you want to drop off the martinis, or you can call your friend over to help."

Oh, okay, that makes total sense now. I knew it was way too good to be true that this auburn wolf would want anything to do with a fat nerd. I tried to avoid thinking of myself that way, but reality hit me hard and I just went straight to negative. He was interested in Syl and he wanted me to introduce them. I guess I made a pretty good wingman, showing off Syl's joking nature. "Sure," I said as I waved for him to come over. "If you want to meet him I can make him carry his own drink." I tried not to let the sadness creep into my face, but it was a real blow to the little confidence I had built up that day.

"I'd love to meet your friends, but can I get your name first? I'm Caine, co-owner and part time bartender of all you see before you." He gestured around the room and then focused back on me for my response. I was so confused. Is he flirting or just doing his job? Is he interested in me?

"I'm Logan, and I'm here to drink," I joked and he chuckled.

"Not here to meet someone?" Caine asked. What a sexy name. *Caine—Caine—Caine,* It just sounded hot and badass. It suited him in his tight black t-shirt over his cut compact frame. It left very little to the imagination. I think I could see his six pack indentations through the fabric.

"Not particularly. I um...I don't have...." Syl walked up and saved me from spewing out nonsense about how I am single for obvious reasons, digging myself into a self deprecating hole. I knew when this night was over I needed to take tomorrow to reset and work on my self image, because it was clearly tanking today.

"Hey Lo –you called and I came." He just couldn't resist an opportunity to make a cum joke. *I guess Caine was right.* That made me giggle and got me out of my head. He continued, "What's wrong, you and your strapping young man can't figure out my fancy drink?"

"Hi Syl," Caine said. "I've probably got a decade on you, but I'll take the compliment. I made your Pink Squirrel, but I think Logan here needs a few extra hands to carry all these drinks to your table."

"Oh Lo, he's hot and helpful. Don't let him get away. I'll grab these and you keep yours. And –we'll see you when we see you." He winked and wandered away.

I couldn't believe Syl just dropped all that insanity and then left me here. "I am so sorry. I can't even blame alcohol because that's just him. I'm just going to take my drink and let you get back to work." I started to slink away, but he called out to me.

"Wait, if you come back to talk to me again later the next round is on me." He winked at me and then went to another customer to get their order.

In a daze, I went back to the table. Devon looked like he was about to burst out of his skin in excitement. I just sunk down in my seat and stared. "I don't get it."

Devon frowned. "Babes – Logan, you have to realize that lots of men will find you attractive."

"Sure, some men do, but never a man as freaking hot as that! Men like that have only ever ignored me or been cruel. I'm not interested in being someone's joke or verbal punching bag. I beat myself up enough as it is." I felt the negativity seep into my bones, but I looked at the bar and Caine was still stealing glances my way.

"Come on now Logan. He talked with you for ten minutes while making four drinks. Do you see him doing that with anyone else? He is very into you." Devon said with an eyebrow waggle. "The way you are talking isn't fair to yourself or him."

Well, I felt sufficiently scolded. I knew he was right. If I was being objective I could see that I had some attractive features and I wasn't an ogre or anything. Not that ogres weren't cool. I just needed to dance and get some courage to go back and talk to him. Liquid courage would have to do, so I slugged back my drink and told Syl they were playing our song. I was going in once it was done.

6

CAINE

Well, that didn't go as planned. I was putting down some heavy game. Not to mention the obvious eyefucking I had been doing all evening. He walked away and I am not sure he'll come back. *Damn, maybe I am losing my luster*. No, Kelly couldn't be right. Besides, I'm not even in the market for a relationship. Am I? I don't know, but this boy isn't just a good fuck or even dinner and a good fuck. He's different. Different from anyone I've ever met, and I don't know why that is. I'll have to spend time figuring that out. Maybe after I solve the puzzle I'll be able to get him out of my head, although the feeling doesn't sit right with me. He was just so confused and beet red from blushing. I wonder if his whole body turns pink when he flushes. He's sexy and has no idea. If he comes back, I'll get straight to the point and ask him out. I don't want to wait around and have him feel awkward and leave without getting his number.

I kept filling orders and casually chatting as the night went on, looking periodically to make sure he didn't leave. I caught him glancing from time to time and even waved stupidly at him once. God, I felt like a kid floundering by the punch bowl at prom. I watched as twinkles dragged him back on the dance floor. He closed his eyes again and I watched him move. I could have kissed the DJ for playing a song that made Logan move his hips like that. I felt my dick twitch at the sight of him. Considering I am in the business of hospitality, it wouldn't look good if I had to adjust myself behind the bar, so I tried to concentrate on setting up Kelly for her big order. "Hey Kelly, have you seen him in here before?"

"Who, the kid dancing with the big guy? He looks like your type," she said, grinning, but I couldn't return her smile. I was sort of shocked. Twinkles was my typical type, so she was right about that, but I didn't really think about "big" being a word to describe Logan, and I was even more surprised that Kelly would say that. She looked at me with her eyebrows furrowed. "What?"

"I'm talking about the 'big guy' actually," I said with air quotes.

"Oh...really. He doesn't seem like someone you'd go for. I didn't mean anything by it. I'm a big girl myself, and he is big, or at least bigger than the twinks and muscle boys you tend to take home."

"I like the way he looks and just watch him dance."

"He's cute, Caine, but I've never seen him in here before. The other guys at his table are regulars. Devon has been coming in on and off for quite a while, but not as much since he met his boyfriend."

"I want to ask him out."

"And ––wait, you mean actually like on a date?"

"Yes Kelly, on a date, and no it's not just because you read me the riot act earlier and called me old. He's different."

"He dances different."

"Kelly!" I shot her the meanest glare.

"Okay--okay, sorry, I was just messing around with you boss. You just surprised me wanting to date anyone. Look, if you like him, what's the problem? You charm the pants off men on a daily basis."

"It didn't work earlier. He sort of turned red and left when I put the moves on him."

" 'Put the moves on him.' Oh my, maybe you are too old or too lame now." Laughing, she continued, "He is different, like you said. Different from the guys you hook up with that think they're hot shit. So a different approach might be needed. Maybe he didn't expect to be hit on." She shrugged.

"He does seem to want to melt into the background when he's not with his friends. I don't think he knows he's hot, and damn if that doesn't make him even more appealing." I paused as I saw Logan walking this way. He looked taller and made eye contact with me.

"Hi."

That was it. He didn't say anything else, but he didn't look away either. "Hey," I said back. I knew I was being weird, but I was just sort of baffled at the difference of the man in front of me. He was rigid and intense, nothing like the blushing bubbly Logan from earlier. The silence went on and the awkwardness was building. Kelly took that moment to elbow me in the back. "Did you come for your free round?" I said finally.

"Um--sure, but you said you wanted me to come back and talk to you?" He made it a question, although he was being direct. I saw him rub his neck and fidget till he realized and put his hands in his pockets. He was so puzzling, but I liked how he could be insecure and still hold his nerve. He was trying to be bold.

"Actually, I didn't want to talk to you," I said, and then asked Kelly to make his drinks for me. Logan's face fell and all the resolve left his body. *Oh fuck*, I took a quick breath. "I actually wanted to get your number and see if you would be available for dinner sometime this week."

His effervescent giggles filled the air. It still sounded so sweet, but I didn't know what to think. *Did he think I was joking? Was he turning me down?* I didn't understand, but the look on his face as he pulled himself together said he didn't get it either. "You're serious?" Logan said. "You want to take me on a date?"

"Yes, I do," I said, simply so there would be no more room for confusion.

"Wh...uh, okay. I have weekends off, but a weeknight could work if the bar needs you. Or it could be a daytime thing?" he said, blinking and bewildered.

"Ok, then, great, how about tomorrow? I think I have a bartender that owes me a shift." I turned to look at Kelly and she nodded. I knew she'd have my back even if Russ couldn't make it.

"Sure––sounds good." Logan looked like he was going to run again, but we exchanged numbers and test texted each other so we could solidify plans later on. I'm not sure that he looked happy when he left, but his big eyes looked earnest. I, however, was on top of the world and couldn't wait till tomorrow night.

7

LOGAN

Panic. I was panicking. I couldn't get Syl out of there fast enough. Tomorrow night–tomorrow–night. How could it be that the hottest guy I have ever seen is going to take me out––on a date––tomorrow night. Why? This was so surreal. What am I going to wear? I needed Syl to come back to my place and help me not spin out of control. I was eager and terrified. I wasn't sure which one of those was making me want to vomit.

"Deep breaths, dear heart. You are working yourself up into a tizzy. Now, I already have you covered. I'm staying over and we are going to pick out your outfit, and if you aren't comfortable in anything, I will take you shopping in the morning. So now the only question is what accessories do you feel best in so we can coordinate?"

"You really are the best. I am a mess, but you always come in to clean me up."

"And I always will, Lo. If you haven't gotten away from me yet it's just not going to happen. Besides, even if you ran away––I'd find you." Syl said in a creepy serial killer kind of way, but it was oddly comforting.

The rest of the night we tried on endless outfit combinations and I felt good about some of my options. Syl insisted that I couldn't make a decision until I hammered out the details of the date with Caine so I would know how dressy or casual to be. I couldn't sleep pondering over what sort of text I would send him in the morning or even what time I should ask. He ran a bar that didn't even close until two in the morning, so I doubted he would be an early bird, but I wanted to make sure I had enough time to get ready. Syl still wanted to take me shopping to keep my mind busy and so I "would have other options for future dates." I love how optimistic he is about everything. I know he believes this will go well and he is already planning our happily ever after, but I just don't think that way, at least not about where I'm concerned. *That's it, table the self doubt. I'm so exhausted.* So I rolled over, listening to Syl snore, and thought about running my hands through Caines dark red hair till I fell asleep.

The next morning, I woke up hearing Syl in the kitchen chiding Hulk for scratching at his leg, and I looked at my phone. Good gosh, it was half past ten and I had a text from Caine! I sprung up and opened the message.

Caine: Hey handsome, when can I pick you up for dinner tonight?

I called Syl into the bedroom, and we planned how long our shopping trip would take and added in the time to get ready. Syl said he had a few relaxing treatments to try that would make me even more gorgeous, so I add that time in too before I reply.

Logan: Anytime after six would work. Where are we going?

Caine: I was thinking italian, maybe Zias? I can make a reservation for seven, so I can pick you up at six. That will give us plenty of time.

Logan: Sounds good :)

Caine: Can't wait ;)

"Holy shit, he winky faced you!" Syl squealed. "That's good, because I knew you were already questioning that smiley."

I texted Caine my address and asked for the general area of the restaurant since it wasn't familiar to me. And that was it. I couldn't contain my smile. "He sounds excited. I've never been to this place before. Have you?"

"Nope, but I'm sure the internet can answer all our questions about the vibe of the restaurant and how absolutely fabulous the ambiance is."

Syl was right. We looked at pictures of the place customers had posted and checked out the social media. It did look fabulous, but not too fancy. There were cozy booths, a small bar, and a rustic brick fireplace as a focal point. It looked small but special, and the menu had amazing dishes like marinated eel in a balsamic glaze and Pizza Pugliese, which as close as I could figure had to do with onions. Some of the menu had italian, but there were still old standbys like spaghetti and meatballs. I mean, how could you go wrong with pasta. *Unless maybe there was more eel involved.*

Syl still wanted to do a little shopping, though, so I got out of my pajamas and gulped down some coffee Syl had made earlier when he was berating my cat, then off to the mall we went. I was actually looking forward to finding some new things to add to my wardrobe; facing the dressing room was a different story, but I knew it would all be worth it when I felt comfortable on my date tonight.

The facials, the spa kind not the jizz kind, (*oh no I was turning into Syl),* and the lotions he had me try after my shower were very relaxing. He kept things light and distracted me everytime he sensed me starting to spiral. We looked through our purchases and decided that I would wear black skinny jeans and a gray tweed blazer with a lightweight cream sweater underneath. It sounds bland as oatmeal, but for me light colors were out of my wheelhouse. Besides, the tweed blazer had some cute maroon elbow patches on it, so that was fun, right? I felt good and I could fidget with the rose gold bangles I put on to go with it. It was getting close to six o'clock, so Syl wished me luck and went on his way. He had plans to go to Devon and Samuel's place for a nice night in. I rolled my eyes at that, thinking how different this weekend would have been if I had convinced Syl to stay in last night. That's when I heard a knock at the door.

8

CAINE

I pulled up outside Logan's apartment building. I picked up a bunch of pink tulips on the way. Dating isn't the norm for me, but I wasn't totally clueless. I wanted to start--whatever this is–off on the right foot. I was taking Logan to one of my favorite places for some amazing food, and then hopefully if things go well maybe we could take a late night stroll on the pier before I drop him home. I will be a one hundred percent gentleman and not plan on 'coming in for a drink' at the end of the date. As much as I want to do all the dirty filthy things my mind can imagine with Logan, I do also want this to last more than one night. I want to learn what makes him laugh.--*And the other noises he might make.* Okay, change of thought, let's get upstairs and get him out of his apartment before I rip his clothes off.

When I get to his door and knock I can feel bubbles in my stomach. Not the good feeling I get when Logan laughs, and I realize I'm really nervous. He opens the door and I practically throw the flowers at him. "For you, handsome. Wow, you look great!" And he did look--stunning. He was all done up in skin tight pants, this sexy librarian jacket, and he had these pretty bracelets stacked up his arm.

"You brought me flowers? They're lovely. I'll just put these in water and then we can go. Did you want to come in for a minute?"

"No! Nope, I'm fine right here if you want to get going." *What the fuck am I doing?* I need to pull myself together. I closed the door, but stayed nearby so that I wasn't tempted to walk up behind him and grab his ass.

"Sure, we can go, just one minute." He grabbed a vase from under his sink and unwrapped the flowers. He seemed so surprised that I got him flowers, and I watched as he smelled the bouquet. He had a huge smile on his face, and the bad bubbles in my stomach started to turn to good. I felt excited to be here with him and less anxious. He noticed I was staring at him and he squeaked. "Ready now––now I'm ready. Good to go––and thank you for the flowers. I forgot to say that before. Oh, and you look amazing. That olive shirt really brings out the flecks of gold in your eyes." He blushed all the way to the tips of his ears. He turned away from me and locked his apartment.

"You're sweet, and thank you. I cleaned up just for you." I felt my mojo coming back. I liked watching him squirm a little. He practically glowed when I teased him. We walked down the three flights of stairs in silence.

I opened up the car door for him and he eased in. I was thinking of things I could ask him as I got in the driver's seat and settled on, "Did you grow up around here?"

"Yeah, not too far from here. Syl and I grew up together about an hour away and decided to move from our small town about six years ago. I practically have to bathe in sunscreen and I am definitely not built for the beach, but I really like it here. How about you?"

"I am a local boy. I grew up here sneaking into bars like mine with fake IDs and spent my early twenties bartending till my friend Emmett wanted to start a business and needed someone with bar experience. Honestly, I think he just didn't want to do it alone, because neither one of us had any idea what we were getting into." We laughed and continued talking about the bar and how Emmett and I got started. I noticed that everytime I asked him a question, he would give a quick answer and usually add some self-deprecating remark before turning the conversation back to me. By the time we arrived at the restaurant, I felt like I had given him my life story in a nutshell, and I knew next to nothing about him. The hostess sat us at a booth in the corner and we looked over the menus. I decided to change the topic to see if I could get him to loosen up a little more. "What do you think you might want to order?"

"So, this is probably the point in the night where I should order a salad and pretend I don't want to eat all the pasta, but chicken parmesan is one of my favorite dishes," he said, smiling, but still sort of self conscious.

"Order whatever you want. I love pasta too, and we already get salad and bread with our meals. The house salad dressing has pesto in it and it's––very–– creamy," I said with a wink, and he answered with one of his bubbly laughs. I liked that he was still willing to order what he wanted, but I hoped he didn't think I was judging him for what he eats.

"Do you think it will be odd years from now if our inside joke involves innuendos about ejaculate? Not that I'm thinking we might be together years from now. I'm sorry." Logan folded in on himself, and I think I started to piece together the puzzle of his personality, and it gave me an idea.

"It's fine, Logan, and I hope we are still joking about ejaculate together when we are old and gray, although for me the gray might come a little faster." This time we laughed together. While it bothered me to think that Logan didn't like the way he looked, his brand of humor wasn't a turn off. I just didn't think his size was a flaw.

"You aren't old or gray, and I'm sorry I am being weird. I swear it is just nerves. You are a very attractive man, and while I like myself, I don't really like my body, so I am a little confused why you asked me out." Well, things took a turn towards heavy, but I liked that he was being honest.

"I asked you out because I think you're damn fine. If I am being honest too, then I will admit that I couldn't take my eyes off you at the bar. You might not like your body, but I do, and I would like to know the parts you do like about yourself too."

"Oh--okay." He was speechless for a few moments, but I think that got the ball rolling. He started telling me about his job at the accounting firm. Logan lit up as he told me about the marketing projects his boss was giving him and the plans he had for the office. The conversation changed to movies we liked, and while I was not nearly as big of a hero buff as Logan, we both liked the latest Venom movie and thought that Syl was crazy for not wanting to watch Ant Man. I found out I owed Syl a thank you for convincing Logan to come to my bar last night.

Logan went to the restroom, and while he was gone, I thought about taking him to an ice cream shop if he wants to walk on the pier after dinner but it closes at nine. We had time to finish our meals, but I wanted to keep an eye on the clock to make sure we wouldn't have to rush. He came back and saw me looking at my watch.

"Listen, if we need to call it an early night, that's okay. I get it," he said hesitantly.

"No! Absolutely not. Sorry, that's not why I was checking the time. I looked at my watch because I wondered if you wanted dessert?" He looked skeptical, but a little less disappointed.

"I don't generally turn down sweets––obviously." Logan gestured down his body.

I grabbed his hand as he was putting it back down on the table and I held it in mine. "Look, I understand that you feel like you need to keep reminding yourself, me, or someone that you like food and that you are a bigger build, but I am very attracted to everything about you, and I'll keep reminding you about that too. I was hoping to take a romantic evening walk with you down the pier to a cute little ice cream shop, that's why I was checking my watch. They have a dulce de leche ice cream and I plan to get a double scoop." I watched his nose crinkle cutely, and he covered his face. My boy was bashful, and damn, it was adorable.

We brought the topic of conversation back to our jobs and friends while we wrapped up dinner. I paid the check and we grabbed our jackets so we could start our venture for dessert. I found myself thinking about other things I wanted to do with Logan. Not just date things or sex, but everyday things like grocery shopping and reading on the couch. I wanted to fast forward through the evening so I could kiss him, but I also wanted us to take our time and stretch it out as long as it could go. I've never felt this way before. In a rush, but also wanting to stand still. It was frighteningly new, but I liked it. I liked Logan and I wanted to know more.

9

LOGAN

This night was magical. Or at least it would be if I would stop putting my foot in my mouth. I didn't want to annoy him with my hang ups. I hated being the funny fat guy. I preferred sarcasm and snark, but for some reason I couldn't let up on myself. It had to be irritating. I was bothering myself. But then he held my hand at dinner and told me all these lovely things I would never use to describe myself. I'm not 'damn fine.' Maybe cute and fluffy, but never fine, and certainly not enough to cuss about.

The air was brisk as we walked, but romantic was right. He had his arm around my shoulders, guiding me down the pier under the moonlit sky with the ocean waves crashing below. Really, how much more needed to happen before I could say I was living in a romantic comedy? The only thing tethering me to reality was my shoes pinching my toes as we walked. I gave him a tight lipped grin as I tried to focus on his story about when the pipe burst at the bar two days before the grand opening. He laughed as he described how his friend Emmett screamed like a howler monkey and demanded the building owner fix the issue before patrons came through the door.

"I have never seen him so angry and aggressive. Needless to say, as soon as we were making a profit and had the means, we bought the property, and now Emmett actually lives upstairs." He looked my way and frowned. "Are you okay Logan?"

"Oh yes, I'm great," I lied. "Isn't it really loud to live above a bar, especially with all the music?"

It is, but most of the loudness comes on the weekends, and we tend to work a lot at night. Em has never been a good sleeper though." He stopped walking and faced me. "You sure you're okay? You look like you're in pain."

"I'm sorry. I just didn't want to ruin the night, and I didn't think about it before, but these shoes aren't really made for walking, just looking cute."

"I didn't even think to say anything when we made plans earlier; I'm sorry. We are almost to the shop, and I know it's chilly, but if you want to walk barefoot on the way back I'll carry your shoes."

"Oh gosh, you're too good to be true, but no, really, I'll be okay. Like you said, we are almost there, and I have some epsom salts and a foot bath calling my name when I get home later." He chuckled and let it go. He was right, we only had to make it past a few more storefronts to get there. It was a sweet mom and pop shop and they had some neat flavors like pb&j and key lime pie. Caine got his double scoop of dulce de leche and I decided on a scoop of german chocolate cake and some classic vanilla. It was all homemade, and I could even see the vanilla bean specks in the ice cream.

"It is probably a little cold to walk and eat this, so how about we sit a bit and you can rest your feet?" I nodded and then watched his eyes roll back in his head as he took his first mouthful of dulce de leche.

I am pretty sure I just saw Caine have a foodgasm, and if that wasn't enough to make my dick take notice, the groan that came from his lips definitely did. He must have watched me staring, possibly drooling. "Eh hem––sorry, this is really spectacular. I can't say it's better than sex, but it is a close second."

I guffawed. "You don't say. Well, from what I witnessed it might have been sex. That was some asmr mukbang sort of fun you were having. I never thought that would be my thing, but you might have me reconsidering." His casual playfulness was so inviting I didn't mind being a little more risque.

"You must have enjoyed the show, because your ice cream is melting and you haven't even tried it. But here, before you do, take a lick." Caine held his cone in front of my face. And yes, I know how that sounds. His words were sensual, and this felt very intimate. I leaned forward and ran my tongue across his ice cream. *Hot damn––that's fucking good.*

"I'm not sure your description is entirely accurate, because in my experience this is way better than sex." I had to hold in a groan of my own. I watched as Caine took another lick and reached his other hand down, appearing to adjust himself.

"I'm not sure you've have good sex then," he joked.

He wasn't wrong. My sex life was pretty limited, and not exactly something I looked forward trying again. It was fumbly, and I always felt like I was in the way of what the guy wanted to do. It usually ended up with me on all fours in the dark worrying about where hands were traveling to. The kissing was nice when it happened, but for the most part it was just sex. We'd finish and they'd leave. Not that I wanted to tell Caine any of this. But then he noticed I wasn't laughing with him.

"I'm not really sure this is great first date chit chat, but I don't really date. In fact, this is the first date I have been on for––god, I don't know how long." He didn't date? Suddenly all the romance went out the window and I imagined this night ending like all of my interactions with men--alone. "Logan? I'm sorry, I don't want to give you the wrong impression. I really don't know what I am doing here. I would blame my lack of a date life on work, but honestly, I was just happy with hook ups."

The only part of that sentence that caught my attention, "Was? You said that like things have changed for you?"

"Well yeah, Logan, it changed when I met you. This is a date. Our first date, in fact, and I am sort of hopeful there will be a second." My brain felt like a ping pong ball going back and forth in my head.

"Wait, I'm confused. What impression were you avoiding? That you aren't good at dating? Because so far you are knocking my socks off, quite literally if I end up walking back barefoot. Besides, I have never really dated either. Guys would have to be interested in me to date me." Caine looked so serious, and I just wanted to rewind to when we were talking about food and movies.

"Logan, I am interested in you, and that's why what I am about to say is going to be a little hard to follow. I hook up a lot, and so far that's all I've wanted, but I don't want to do that with you. Knowing now that neither one of us dates and we are navigating new ground, I wanted to be clear that I don't want to have sex with you tonight."

"Okay..."

"I have hopes that this can be different, but that means that I need to be different. We can find what dating our way means, but I think taking you to bed so soon would be a mistake. I'm not saying we should take things slow, because, honestly, I don't think I can do that for long, but I just want to leave you tonight with a kiss and enjoy the wait. Did that make any sense?"

"So--if I am following you. You want me, but not now? And I'm going to get a kiss and more dates?" He eagerly nodded. "Wait, this is all under the assumption that I was going to try and sleep with you tonight." I said raising my brow at him, but I couldn't stop the grin that was forming.

Visibly relieved that I was teasing him, he said, "Well, clearly you've been seducing me all evening."

I burst out laughing and all the tension left the air. "I am the farthest thing from a seducer, but just to protect your virtue, maybe we should both agree to at least stick to the three date rule?"

"I'm not sure I can resist your charms that long, but we can stick with that while we figure out the rest." The flirtatiousness came back into our conversation, and we kept things light as we finished our mostly melted ice cream, which of course still tasted phenomenal. We tossed our trash, and I was seriously considering taking off my shoes for the trip back when...

"Wh...what are you doing?" I asked as Caine was standing with his back to me trying to put my arms around his neck.

"You look miserable just thinking about walking to the car and the temperature really is dropping so--piggy back is the only option." My eyes widened. Not that he could see them.

"Are you insane? You are not carrying all of this the whole way back to your car."

"I won't drop you. I promise. It's not even a half mile." Caine said it like it was nothing. *'I carry overweight men home all the time.* Hahaha,' I imagined him saying.

"I don't think you're going to drop me. I'm going to squish you."

"Nah, it'll be fine. Trust me." And he turned around and reached for my arms again. Disoriented, I let him, and then good golly my feet left the ground and he hoisted me up on his firm back. "Just hold on and enjoy the ride." Caine said in a playful tone.

I held on tight. Maybe a little too tight, but he didn't say anything more. This was mortifying. His hands were all over my thighs and way too close to my ass. Pressed so close to him, my body stuck to his leather jacket like a suction cup. If I wasn't so embarrassed, I would probably be rock hard. He was only a few inches taller than me, but he was built, and it really didn't seem like carrying me was a struggle. The wind picked up as he walked along, so I tucked my chin to his neck and breathed in his scent. Caine smelled like expensive cologne and basil. My bangles jingled as he picked up the pace, and I felt wetness on my face and realized his neck was starting to bead with sweat. We were getting close to the car, and as reluctant as I was to do this, I was sad to lose this overwhelming feeling of acceptance.

He released my legs, and I slid down his body with no grace whatsoever. I let him go and he turned around and put his hands lightly on my waist. "Not too bad, was it?" He quietly said, gazing at me.

"No, not at all." I managed to eke out. I wanted to apologize or say something witty to take away my discomfort from earlier, but I found I liked the mood. He didn't need an apology, and I had nothing to be sorry for.

He moved in and pressed his lips to mine. It was gentle and sweet, but his tongue soon smoothed over them and I let him in. We kissed slowly, and as stirring as it was, it was full of hope, not hunger. We drifted for moments, but then the wind blew through and we parted. Caine opened my car door again, and we rode to my place in a comfortable silence. I didn't let him walk me up. I didn't want to get carried away and wake up with regret, so we said goodnight in the car, and he leaned over the console and placed a kiss on my forehead before I unbuckled and went upstairs.

10

CAINE

I have never felt this good in my life. It was like a mellow high I felt deep in my bones. I didn't want to go home yet. I couldn't just lay in bed awake for hours, so I went to the bar. I knew a drink and a talk with Emmett would set me back on track and help me think of some message to send Logan to finish our night.

Emmett was in the back office on his laptop when I arrived. He seemed surprised to see me. "Over so soon?"

"Em, it was amazing. How can it feel this good when I didn't even fuck him?" Emmett wasn't even shocked by my crudeness. He was used to my cursing and he did a fair bit of that too.

"You didn't have sex. I'm impressed." He smirked. "No offense, but I figured you would still sleep with him even if you wanted to see him again. Now I need to hear, man. You have a dreamy look in your eyes."

I recounted the evening's events in as much detail as I could. Emmett laughed at the piggy back story and swooned when I told him about how I kissed Logan and said goodnight. "Caine, I have to admit

I'm a little jealous. It sounds like the perfect night, and your man sounds pretty special." Emmett nudged my shoulder and then he got up to pour us a drink. "So, when do you see him again?" he asked.

"I don't know. We didn't exactly make plans. The end of the night is all——fuzzy."

"Man, you have it bad, but if this boy is as insecure as you say he is, then a vague mention of a second date with no real details is going to make him question everything." It made sense and I could just picture Logan pacing in his apartment overanalyzing or calling Syl for reassurance. I didn't want to make him suffer, and I wanted to see him as soon as possible so I texted him.

Caine: You know I can't wait to see you again. So I need you to put me out of my misery. Are you free tomorrow?

Logan: I had a wonderful time. I want to see you too. I have no plans at all tomorrow except to meet up with Syl after his shift at the beauty store.

Caine: I can't promise it will be romantic, but I wouldn't think you were a creepy stalker if you came and kept me company at work. Sunday can be pretty slow, and Syl can come by too. What do you think?

Logan: I'd love to stalk you. What time?

Caine: We open at noon, so whenever works. I'll be there all day.

Logan: I'll see you at noon. Goodnight x

Caine: Sweet dreams Logan

I smiled as I sent the last message and was so glad he was willing to come into the bar. I rarely got a weekend off, and I knew he had his office job during the week. It didn't feel right to wait so long. I told Emmett about our plan and he was happy for me, although a little less so when I told him he'd have to meet Logan. I knew not to take it personally, but I just wanted my friend to meet my——well, my date?

No, that sounds strange. I wanted him to meet my Logan. We talked a while longer till I thought I could go home and actually sleep.

The next morning was pretty dull in comparison to the night before. I got out of bed and hopped in the shower and wondered how Logan spent his mornings. Was he an early riser, or would he be having a nice lazy Sunday if I hadn't asked him to meet me? I soaped my body and imagined Logan waking up beside me with morning wood and the way I bet he'd cover his face as I ran my hand down his body to help relieve the pressure. While I don't think the piggy back ride was exciting for him last night, I could still feel his bulge on my lower back. I grabbed my cock and teased the tip as the water ran down my body. I think of Logan's tongue running around my crown and then wrapping his lips around the shaft to sink down slowly, then sliding back up, sticking his tongue out to brush along the veins of my cock. I licked my lips and bit hard as I felt my balls tighten. With just a few more strokes I painted the shower tiles, thinking how much better this would be if Logan could lick it up like he did that ice cream cone.

Back to reality, I got dressed in my Built Bar shirt and jeans. I ran some mouse through my hair for some bounce and to keep it off my face. I have never been a daily shaver, so I would let a little scruff grow for a few days. Last night was great, but I knew not every moment with Logan would be button ups and candlelit dinners. Most nights I dragged myself home worn out and sort of scuzzy. Bars are messy, and I usually smelled like beer and body odor by the end of a shift. Not that I wouldn't put in the effort to give Logan what he deserves, but I did want him to see me and not just fall in love with the best parts. *Geez, love, what the fuck is my mind jumping to?* This date would be low key since we were still getting to know each other, and I hoped the relaxed vibe of a Sunday at the bar would help keep things flowing.

I got to the bar at ten o'clock to run the staff meeting and change out the kegs we kicked last night. Russ was behind the bar with me today, and since it would probably stay fairly slow, I would have plenty of time to hang out with Logan. I was cutting up fruit and didn't see him walk up with Emmett.

"Am I your first customer?" He said demurely.

"You are indeed, and my favorite so far." I teased.

Emmett chimed in. "Well I'm glad to see he doesn't just like messing with me."

"Oh no, I'm an equal opportunity ball buster." I quipped back. That made Logan giggle and those good bubbles fizzed in my veins at that sound. He had long strands of silver dangling from his ears with a black velvet long sleeve shirt that had an intricate floral pattern stitched into the material. It fit him loosely, but his gray jeans fit snug the whole way down to comfortable looking shoes. I bet those pants hugged his ass in the back. I was tempted to ask him to do a spin for me.

I must have had a stupid look on my face, because Emmett said. "Wipe that stupid look off your face and get to work. Your boy is thirsty." He covered his mouth with his hand while he cackled. "Oh, and Logan, it was nice to meet you and I hope to see a lot more of you around here. Drinks are on Caine." He held out his hand for Logan and they shook. I was glad Emmett made an effort to come out and meet him. I would have to set something more private up for them to interact so he could loosen up more, but I had first dibs on Logan's time.

"Gin and tonic or something else?" I asked Logan, hoping the alcohol will work in my favor and get him talking and at ease.

"Oh sure, you remembered." He pinked and I melted.

"I know all my regular's orders, and I am assuming that's going to be what you are." He nodded and smiled as I made his drink then poured a soda for myself. I walked around the bar with the drinks and asked Russ to holler if he needed me. He gave me a salute and I guided Logan to the booth in the back. I set the drinks down and placed my hand behind his ear to lift his face up for a kiss. His lips were soft, and I only lingered for a second before I pulled back and sat down.

"Mmmm––Hi," he said.

"Hey," I murmured, now very aware of the eyes of my staff watching us. They've seen me flirt shamelessly and leave with guys, but I've never actually done anything here at the bar. I took a gulp of my coke as I sat down and looked at Logan to see if he felt uncomfortable, but he seemed to not notice there was anyone else in the bar.

Logan broke the silence. "I'm glad we could meet so soon. I didn't want to have to wait till we both had time off again. I can imagine with running a business you don't get designated days off on a regular basis."

"You're right, this place takes up most of my time––but I also never really had a reason to schedule myself days off before, and now I do."

"I'm the reason?" Logan asked sheepishly.

"Of course!" I said without hesitation.

He gave me a happy sigh, and we sipped and slipped into conversation about our families. It surprised me that Logan didn't really stay in touch with his family. He said his mom passed away when he was thirteen and he and his dad were never close. He really had no family to speak of apart from Syl, who was like a brother to him, and the close group of friends he has gathered over the past few years. Similarly, I had no siblings or father in my life, but I still saw my mom regularly. It was just the two of us growing up. I told him a few stories, like the time I brought head lice home from school and we stayed home and played board games all day with our heads slathered in mayonnaise. Or when I came out to her when I was twenty and she didn't bat an eye.

"We had cake for dinner that night and she asked me if I was seeing anyone." I loved that memory. "I did, however, have to sit through a very lengthy safe sex talk and found out my mom knew way too much about anal sex and ass play," I told him with a shudder. "Ma can be pretty prim and proper, but incredibly supportive. Too supportive, maybe to a fault."

He sat there laughing his ass off. When he finally caught his breath he added, "The internet is an incredibly powerful thing, and in the wrong hands it can do great evil."

"You are such a nerd." I picked his hand up off the table and gave it a kiss. "Just a fucking cute nerd with a tight ass."

"Oh stop--" He was flustered and picking imaginary lint from his velvet shirt. Logan really was not good at taking a compliment. I hoped that I could help change that with enough time. "If anyone has a tight ass at this table it's you. I'm just a chunky nerd."

"Logan, come on..." but he cut me off.

"No Caine, it's okay. I might not like my body, but I like myself. I know me and I'm never going to have abs or any body parts that don't jiggle." He shrugged his shoulders. "I've tried to lose weight and I just never felt good. It would stick for a while, but I always went back to this. I know I'm alright. I've attracted men before, just never enough for them to stick around." I looked at him and saw him look so defeated. I knew a quick subject change or a joke would be the next thing to leave his lips. "The truth is I'd rather have a nutter butter than be someone's fantasy." He gave me a sad smile that barely moved his cheeks.

"I know you won't believe me, but you have been my fantasy. In the shower this morning, in fact. You don't need to change to make me happy. You are smart, funny, a little nerdy, and very sexy to me." I knew he was hurting so I scooted over to his side of the booth and held him to my side. "I have been with lots of men. I probably hurt some of them because I didn't want more. The fact that you have been through that kills me, but that also means that you were free for me now when we are both ready. I can't tell you where we are headed, but I promise that I want more with you---and sex."

He snorted. "You're such a horndog--but thank you. I want more too--and sex. So I guess that means date number three is on the horizon?"

"Most definitely. I have to work some extra shifts because there are some events happening this month, but the first moment I'm free I'm all yours." I kissed his temple and pushed his drink a little closer to him. I felt like he could use it.

That was the moment I saw Syl walking towards us with a Pink Squirrel in hand. "I just had that hunky barman make me a drink and he said it was on you loverboy. Are you trying to get on my good side by plying me with alcohol?"

"Only if it will work, Sparkles," I said deadpan.

"Hah. Oh, it will," he said amusedly, sliding into the booth to give Logan a hug.

"I'll be right back. You two play nice." Logan walked off towards the restroom.

Syl glared at me with a look that made my blood freeze. All sass and kindness left his face. "Listen closely, because you only get one warning. You better not hurt him. He jokes around, but his armor is weak, and you could damage him so easily. You have no idea how far he has come from growing up in small town, going to school in a cornfield, and being the chubby gay kid. It was hell for me, but he took way more of it than I did. If you don't cherish him, I will come back and blow body glitter in your face. That shit will blind you!" *Geez, Sparkles has some serious claws.*

"In all honesty, Syl, we are very new, and neither one of us has had a relationship before. I do have good intentions towards Logan, and I wouldn't want him any other way than how he is. I know he is insecure––he isn't that good at hiding it. I would never want to cause him any pain. You're Logan's family, and I really do want you to like me, because I like him."

"Well, you have brains and brawn in a nice neat package. That's good. I would hate to have to hurt you, especially when you make a better Pink Squirrel than the scorching hot young guy at the bar."

"To be fair, that drink hasn't been popular since before he was born." I was relieved I saw Logan on his way back to us.

"Touché, sir. Now not a word. He hates when I mother him." I didn't believe that for a second. Logan needed to be surrounded by people who protect that fragile part of him. He came to sit back down in the booth and eyed us wearily.

"What did I miss? Why do I sense tension?" He looked at Syl with a raised brow.

"What?" Syl drew out the syllables, putting on a hurt expression. "All we were doing was chatting. It's been a lovely time."

"Chatting about what?" Logan asked, unimpressed by the show he was putting on.

"Kale," Syl said nonchalantly. Logan looked skeptical, but I nodded along, backing him up. Finally Syl scoffed. "Yes, kale, it's like the new superfood in everything. I couldn't even find a smoothie this morning that didn't have it." Logan knew it was all a lie and I was sure he would ask later about what went down between us when he went to the bathroom, but he let it drop and I threw in my two cents on the vegetation.

"I don't mind kale and all the health stuff as long as I can have a good greasy cheeseburger too."

"I think kale people tend to avoid that combo. Maybe they would have, like, a portabella burger to go with their kale." This got Logan going and I enjoyed watching his face distort at the various kale creations Syl teased him with.

"Really? I mean, I like veggie burgers, and kale isn't--that bad, but I hate it when people try to make it sound amazing or like a treat. Because honestly, you can fry it in butter and serve it up by the plateful, but kale will never be a guilty pleasure." And that's how we spent twenty minutes talking about greens and progressed into other strange topics from there.

The afternoon went great. Logan and Syl shared more about their adventures growing up and we all laughed quoting lines from tv shows we've seen. By the end I realized that no one under thirty watched Doogie Howser, and I got a recommendation for a cream that 'would help my crows feet.' Syl did get his hand slapped for that one, and it felt good that Logan was looking out for me too.

Eventually the bar did get busy, so I had to leave Logan and Syl to their own devices. The two of them could take on the world together, and that made me happy. They had a few rounds and lots of water then said goodbye. I didn't want him to go. I knew it would be a while before I could see him again. Apart from some slow Sundays, the bar really was short staffed, and we were booking lots of local talent to keep the newer club crowd happy. I decided to go up to Emmett's before I went home so I could remind him to set up some interviews for fresh blood so we could have the opportunity to take time off.

"Knock knock, Em, I'm coming in." I saw him scrubbing his kitchen sink. The whole place smelled like bleach. "You ok, Em?" He stopped.

"Yeah, I'm fine. I just haven't done a deep clean of the kitchen in a while." I was pretty sure he did that Tuesday. He didn't get like this often, but he must have had a hard day. I knew I didn't want to pressure him about the interviews right now. I would save that for another time.

"Everything is ship shape and Russ is just finishing his side work for the first shift tomorrow. I'll lock up on my way out."

"Wait--Caine- how did your date go? Logan seemed nice. I'm not sure if you prepped him, but he didn't stare much." Emmett pulled at his rubber gloves to take them off then joined me to sit at the island.

"He definitely wasn't staring, and yes, I mentioned your Bells Palsy, because I told him all about you and how we started the bar."

"It went well, though--you'll see him again?" I saw him trying to flex the muscles in his face and I knew he was hoping for good news.

"Yeah, it went pretty great. His friend threatened me with bodily harm and I feel really old, but I really liked spending time with them. I didn't set a specific date with Logan, though, because I know we have a lot of performances coming up."

Emmett's left brow crinkled. "He didn't seem disappointed about not going out this Friday?"

"No, not exactly, I told him as soon as I could get some time I would spend it with him. Why?"

"It's Valentine's Day, Caine. I know you are not used to being a boyfriend, but one generally makes special plans that day."

"Fuck..." I ran my fingers through my hair a few times. "I had no idea. Who the hell starts a relationship a week before Valentine's Day?" He didn't even say anything. "That's a Friday, though, and I'm pretty sure we have a new act coming in for the weekend that will need contracts and set up done. Not to mention the sound checks and lighting planning. He'll be so bummed. Two dates and I'm already blowing it." I banged my head into the counter. "He's going to think I'm a thoughtless asshole."

"Calm down, I'll handle it."

"You'll what?"

"I'll fucking handle it. This is your first Valentine's Day and Logan deserves a nice night with you. It's important and I've never seen you take an interest in any guy like this. You are clearly head over heels for him, and it's only been two damn days."

I knew the discomfort it would cause him to have to run that show by himself and interact with strangers. I would stay at the bar as long as I could. There was also a huge possibility that Emmett would lose his nerve and back out. He meant well, but his anxiety would go through the roof. I didn't want to get Logan's hopes up, so I thought I'd keep it a surprise and have a romantic back up plan in case I had to stay. I was so excited, though; Emmett was right about how far gone I already was for Logan. It was crazy going from never feeling anything past friendship for any man to thinking about a future with Logan.

"I owe you so much, man. I don't know what I will do to make it up to you, but you don't know how much I appreciate this." My mind started racing with ideas to make our first Valentine's Day special.

11

LOGAN

So jobs suck. Everything was going fine and I was making a really good impression with my marketing proposals, but it was all just so slow. Caine worked nights and I couldn't stay out at the bar all night with work the next day. We texted everyday, sometimes every hour. We messaged about how our days were going, local happenings in the area, and then ventured into random messages with memes and pictures of food we were eating or drinks he made. Every day we said good morning and at the end of the day we said goodnight.

He still hadn't told me when we would have our third date, and Syl thought it was absolutely horrible that we didn't have Valentine's plans, but I understood and it was fine. Friday rolled around and I decided to wear a new wine colored jacket to work with my jeans. It was a special occasion, and Syl did want me to take baby steps, so I snapped a picture of me in it and sent it to him with the caption 'heartbreaker.' He replied a minute later.

Syl: Wow, love really changes a man. You look fabulous honey. Btw sending this to Sammy and Dev ;)

Syl: Oh and HAPPY VALENTINES DAY in case that lunkhead doesn't say it to you.

Logan: I got my good morning text and he sent me a funny video. I know he's really busy. He has been working ridiculous hours all week.

Syl: MmmmHmmm

Logan: Really Syl it's fine. This is so new and that's a lot of pressure to put on it. I mean it is our third date ;) ;)

Syl: All the more reason he should wine and dine you then rip your clothes off.

Logan: NO. Besides work has been busy for me too, and so Caine knows I'm looking forward to a nice quiet night with a movie or a book and some take out.

Syl: I can cancel my plans and come over.

Logan: Please don't. I'm glad you have a date. Besides I am willing to give up a made up greeting card holiday one day for more time with him the rest of the year.

Syl: You shouldn't have to give anything up. He could at least acknowledge the day with a text or something. Anywho, I gotta work. <3 bye

I know he was just looking out for me and I liked it, but really this Valentine's hurt way less than any of the other ones I spent single. I might be alone tonight, but I knew he was out there thinking of me every now and then. I had been telling myself all this and more throughout the week, and I knew it's all true. The idea of our third date, thee date, happening on our first ever Valentine's- it made my skin crawl. We wanted to take it slow–ish and that would be the opposite. I might be falling faster than Caine, but I wasn't going to do anything to jeopardize what we had growing.

The work day went pretty quick. Someone made red velvet cupcakes and put them in the breakroom for everyone, and I got lots of "You look great" and "Wow, Logan" for wearing some color today. I think I even got a wolf whistle when I went to grab a coffee at break. *Syl might actually have been right.* I did feel better. I heard from Caine around four o'clock, and he was swamped at work with a new band coming in for the weekend. I let him know that I was wrapping up at work and looking forward to a nice comfy movie night. I was hoping I would still get a goodnight text later even though he was busy.

When I got home I gave Hulk a special can of seafood feast and gave her some love. She wolfed down the food so fast and then looked at me with her big green eyes. "One would think I starve you, crazy cat." I scratched her ears and ran my nails down her back to her tail. She turned and mewed up at me, trying to paw my nose. "No, I'm not giving you any more, but I'm glad you liked it." I left Hulk sitting on the kitchen counter and went to shower and change into pajamas. A special night called for the comfiest of clothes, so I put on my cloud pj bottoms and chubby unicorn tee with the cutest baby rhino on it. Devon bought it for me at a thrift shop in town as a joke one day, but it quickly became one of my favorite things. I slipped my feet into my fuzzy croc slippers and was all set for a chill night on the couch. Then I heard a knock at my door.

"Syl, I told you I would be fine tonight. You better not have canceled yo…" I immediately froze when I opened the door and saw Caine standing there with a giant bouquet and lots of bags. "Wha––what are you doing here?!?" I beamed as he leaned in to kiss me.

"Happy Valentine's Day, sweetheart. Are you surprised?" he asked as he placed the flowers and bags on the coffee table. He looked me up and down with a smirk on his very amused face. "Well, aren't you fucking adorable." It hit me that I *was* surprised, and Caine was seeing me in quite possibly the most unattractive outfit in the known world. I uselessly covered my body up with my two hands.

"I——wasn't expecting you, obviously. I'm just going to go in the back and change."

"Don't you dare. I love everything about it. Are you wearing orange crocs?" he said as he grasped me around my upper arms.

My whole face heated in embarrassment. "They're slippers actually, and really comfy. I thought I was going to be ALONE on the couch tonight, so I was just..."

"There's a rainbow baby rhino on your shirt. I need to raise my loungewear game, because there is no way to compete with that." My heart melted. He was laughing, but it wasn't mean spirited. "You are the most adorkable twink I've ever seen."

"I'm no twink; twinks are small and cute. Men usually classify me as a bear."

"Bear!?" Looking confused, "I could be wrong, but you don't appear to have the fur to back that claim up. You don't look like you have a lick of hair on you. I might have to check to be sure——" He moved his hand to my chest, running it down my belly to the bottom of my shirt. I backed away from him and walked over to the big bunch of roses he brought.

"Um——these are beautiful," I said awkwardly. "How are you here right now? I thought you had to work." I tried peeking in the bags he brought, but everything was closed up tight.

Caine coughed and I saw him palm his dick to adjust. I'm pretty sure he wanted me to look, so I kept glancing at his bulge while he spoke. "I did, but a little birdie named Emmett not only reminded me about the date, he also volunteered to cover for me so I could spend it with you. I would have said something sooner, but I wasn't totally sure Emmett wouldn't back out. He has a lot of social anxiety. I have no regrets, though, because I would have hated to miss you in your pjs. I do lose some romance points for not realizing Valentine's Day was this week, but I never had to pay attention to it before."

"Really? That's so kind of him. Will he be okay handling things––um, face to face?" I asked, not sure exactly how to phrase it. From what Caine told me about his friend, this seemed like it would be a nightmare for him.

"I did a lot of prep to get things started this week and left him in a good place. He definitely isn't keen on the idea, but he wouldn't let me miss this time with you."

"Wow, we should do something nice for him."

"Hmmm. 'We,' huh? I like that," Caine said. I blushed. Red was becoming a permanent color for me in his presence. I found I liked the sound of 'we' too. I thought that would make things weird between us, but it was natural. *'Us,' there I go again, and now we're a 'we' even in my mind.*

"Yeah, me too." I blinked. "Let me go put these in some water, and then we can––something. I–– I'm assuming you have some sort of a plan for the evening, and I hope it doesn't involve leaving the house if you don't want me to change."

I left the room and went into the kitchen, saw that Hulk really did eat too fast, because she had puked on the floor and was now probably in hiding. I cleaned up the mess and then got a vase for the roses. They really were beautiful. I felt so special that he wanted to surprise me and made this scheme to get me alone at my home. But I didn't even like him touching my stomach through my shirt. How am I supposed to be naked in front of him?

12

CAINE

I knew showing up at his place unannounced had the possibility of backfiring, but I hoped the cozy night I had planned would make up for the initial embarrassment Logan had for being in his pajamas. It was certainly worth the risk. I was so glad I got the chance to see him comfortable in his environment. I hoped I would get to know a lot more about him tonight. I brought all of the Avenger and the Thor movies for a marathon. I didn't mention it to him yet, but Em was going to cover the whole weekend for us to be together. I definitely noticed how skittish Logan was once I touched his stomach, and I figured he would be a little apprehensive to let me get close again. I'm sure we'd have to talk, and I'd find a way to reassure him. He had to realize that I was crazy about him and his body.

I sat on his couch and started unpacking the bags of snacks and chinese I brought to go with our sexy hero movie marathon when I saw what looked like a dust bunny under the coffee table. Upon closer inspection, I realized it was the tail of a tiny cat. I bent down to look, and the gray fur ball stared back at me with its head tilted and it's green eyes wide.

"Oh, I hope you aren't allergic; that's Hulk," Logan said as he brought the roses to place on a bookshelf next to his entertainment center. I smile at the thought of him naming the itsy bitsy cat after one of the biggest badasses in hero history. He really is too cute for words.

I blinked at him. "That little mouse is named Hulk?"

"Well yeah, I know she's puny, but she's got a big heart, and don't doubt she'll go green on you in the middle of the night when she jumps on your face or takes a swipe at your nipple." He looked so handsome as the blush in his cheeks bloomed bright red.

"So I'll be staying over then? Well, if I am to get the full Hulk experience." Logan looked like he wanted to tuck into his t-shirt like a turtle, but eventually he breathed deep and nodded.

"I--I'd like that, if you want to?"

"There's nothing I'd like more. I've wanted to get you in bed since I laid eyes on you. We can save that for later though. Let's get our relaxing night in started. I brought a selection of movie snacks and some of the movies we talked about." I couldn't stop saying 'we,' but it felt nice.

"I do sort of have an obsession. I guess you figured that out." I nodded as I pointed around the living room to the various posters and figurines. I knew before getting a good look at his place. If I ever wanted to get him talking after he'd clam up, all I needed to do was bring up a superhero and his mouth would hit the ground running. "This is really sweet Caine, thank you."

We settled in and ate dinner, laughing as villains made terrible plots to take over the city and the underdogs saved the day in typical heroic fashion. We put on a new movie, and I moved in closer to Logan and placed my arm around his shoulder. I felt him tense a bit, but it didn't last long. I rested my face on his head and smelled his sweet citrus shampoo. Before I could make another move, Hulk crashed the party and nestled herself on Logan's lap, kneading the fuzzy fabric of his cloud patterned pjs. I would think she was sweet if she wasn't cock blocking me right now. So instead I started to ask him about the fuzzy feline that thwarted my plans.

"Does she do any tricks?" I asked as he scratched her head.

"She's a cat--she poops in a box and leaves hair everywhere. Have you never had a pet before?" He shifted to look at me, and the kitten flicked her tail and scurried off his lap to jump on the bookshelf to run her face against the flowers. "Hulk, if you knock those flowers over I'm locking you out of the bedroom tonight." She didn't even look his way.

"That might be good anyway. Wouldn't want to pollute her mind with all the depraved acts we are going to do." Logan gave a weak laugh. "It's ok if you aren't ready, or if we need to throw out the three date rule. Remember, we are making it up as we go."

"No, it's not that. I--I'm just nervous. I'm no virgin, but my sex life hasn't exactly been full of adventure. In fact, it's been pretty terrible. I've been with four guys, and it's always been the same. In the dark and strictly business, so to speak."

"Baby, I can promise you sex with me won't be like that."

"That's sort of why I'm worried." He couldn't meet my eyes, but I just let him talk and held his hands. "I know you're going to want to touch--all of me --and that's not..." He just stopped, so I tried to piece together where he was going.

"You mean you don't want me to touch your body, or you don't want me to touch your stomach?"

"No! I want you to touch me. I want it to be different, better, but I don't... It's just, have you ever been with a guy like me? You know, bigger, with folds and cellulite? I might have lumps and bumps that you aren't used to."

"Hey, look at me. I want every part of you. I am not perfect and neither is any man I have ever been with. Sex is fun. I am going to be thinking how good it's going to feel to be inside you and how many times I can make you cum." Logan gulped.

"Well, if you keep saying things like that to me you might have to start counting."

"Good, you have youth on your side, so we can play till you're ready to go again." I sat up and pulled my shirt off over my head. I leaned in to nuzzle his neck and nip at his ear while I started to unbutton my pants.

"Oh shit Caine." I grabbed his face and kissed him hard. I needed him to feel how hungry I was for him, to leave his thoughts in his head and be with me. I lifted up his cute as fuck shirt and bent down to pepper kisses on his torso. Logan fought to get his shirt over his head and I licked a trail up to his nipple. It was then I found out why Hulk had her name. That fucking furball picked that moment to launch herself off the bookshelf and onto my back.

13

LOGAN

This was the single hottest moment in my life. It was all so incredible. Caine was voracious and somehow he had an appetite for me. I resisted trying to cover my midsection when he lifted my shirt. I needed to trust that he knew what he wanted. His lips tickled as they touched my belly, and right as I felt his tongue blaze a trail to my chest, I heard a shriek.

"Oh my gosh Caine are you okay?" I saw Hulk leap off Caine to the back of the couch and down the hall. I tried to get up and look at his shoulder, but he put his hand up in a gesture for me to wait.

"It's fine; I don't think she drew any blood," he said as he rolled his shoulder.

"I--am--so--sorry." I couldn't believe it. This was going to ruin everything.

"It's fine Logan, just bad timing, but maybe we should take it to the bedroom and lock the door." He chuckled and his lips still looked swollen from our kiss.

"You still want to stay––and have sex." I was shocked.

"I always want to have sex. I won't be able to get enough of you. And of course I want to stay. Your cat isn't going to keep me away. I told you sex is supposed to be fun, and once you get past the initial animal attack, this is pretty funny."

I stood up and reached out for his hand. I realized I wasn't wearing a shirt and felt self conscious, but then Caine took my hand and gazed into my eyes, so I guided him to my bedroom. His jeans were hanging off his hips, and I could see his black underwear band peeking out. I followed his thin happy trail with my eyes up to lean muscles. He was built. I didn't know it was possible to be so stacked without an ounce of excess bulk. His arms and shoulders were covered in light freckles that spread and became more sparse as they reached his chest. I wanted to run my tongue over them and take on the impossible task of counting them all. I wouldn't even mind starting over every time I missed one.

I stepped towards him, pulled down his zipper, and helped his pants find the floor. I had no idea what I was doing, but I really wanted to do it. Before I could overthink, I slid my hand in his briefs and grabbed his cock. He was big, thick, and hard. It felt like warm cast iron in my hand. Caine's hands moved to his hips and slipped the briefs down his legs. My hand held on as his dick bobbed back up towards his stomach. I should call it the Hulk. *No, that's too confusing.* Thor's hammer? Yes, that's exactly what it was, and his hot, heavy hammer was going to nail me to the bed tonight.

"Stroke me, baby, my cock wants you so bad," Caine whispered in my ear as he stepped in to hold me.

"Caine, I––uh..." I couldn't speak; it felt so good to touch him. All I could think about as my hand moved along his shaft was how much it would stretch me as it went inside. I wanted that so much. "Please––I need you." Caine's hands ran lightly across my side up to clasp my back and pull me in closer. My hand left his cock so it was trapped between our bodies.

"We have to get the rest of these clothes off you then." He kept kissing me softly, and somehow the drawstring to my bottoms came undone, revealing my green and white striped boxer briefs. "That's hot. I think stripes are my new favorite." He slipped a hand inside the band to grip my ass. "Mmm, or this might be my new favorite thing."

My hands raked his back, and I felt the lumps and bumps of his body too. I kissed the freckles on his shoulders and the tips of my fingers reached the dip at the base of his spine. Caine bent to pull my boxers off and his fingers felt like fire as they trailed up my thighs to my dick.

"Oh, my...haahh. Holy hell." He gripped me firmly, squeezing and releasing, milking the tip of my cock. I couldn't take much more of this. I wanted more than just friction. I wanted to feel him pulsing inside me.

"There's so much I want to touch. I don't know where to start, baby. You have to tell me what you want." I couldn't think in words, and I certainly couldn't say what was in my head. "Logan, tell me, do you want me to fuck you or suck you?"

"Oh god--fuck me. Caine, please fuck me." I was begging and I'd say whatever he wanted as long as he would stick his dick in me. I never wanted anything more, never needed anyone more.

"Lay face down on the bed. I need to get you ready." I sprawled across the bed and Caine placed the pillows under my hips and gave me one for my head. He pulled a pack of lube and a condom from--somewhere-- and put it beside me. *I hadn't even thought I couldn't th*.... He licked the crease below my ass as his thumbs ran up the middle, parting my cheeks. "I'm going to rim you and open your hole for me."

I garbled some sort of nonsense, and he started lapping at my pucker. His hands mauled my backside and I clutched the sheets. "Ahhuuuhh nahh god–" I felt his tongue wriggle in my entrance and it sent me writhing. It was the strangest sensation; it made me want to run, but I also wanted it deeper. The latter won out, and I pushed my ass back to his face, my cock rubbing against the mattress. The bristly stubble from his face scratched at my cheeks as he worked me deeper. His tongue left me and I felt depleted. All my muscles let go and went limp on the bed. I was his and couldn't even begin to worry as his hands caressed up the folds of my sides.

"Your skin feels so creamy." He rubbed my shoulders, but I couldn't be more relaxed and wanting. His hands left me and I felt the lube drip down my crease. His first finger slipped right in, and I instantly raised up on my elbows to push back. Caine's other hand was around my neck as he kissed my nape gently. A second finger entered and followed the first to sweep across my prostate. Caine reveled in my moans and whispered hot nothings deep in my ear. I needed to get control. I needed to slow down or this would be done.

"Caine, I'm ready."

"For what?" I exhaled and tried to pull away before I could peak. He held me to him but removed his vexatious fingers. "Breath, baby, and tell me you want my cock inside you."

I drew in air as he hugged me to him. I felt some sense within the sensation, so I said, "I want your cock. I want it inside me. Please fuck my ass." He laughed and pressed kisses on my back as he laid me down on the pillows. I heard the foil ripping and imagined him rolling the condom on his long cock.

"Your wish is my command, dirty boy." His dick teased my hole and and I moved to meet it. He didn't make me wait. His hips moved slowly as his head stretched past my ring. He was thick, but it didn't hurt. I focused on different parts of my body and tried to predict where his hands would skim next, but every part of me felt embraced. He bottomed out in me, ran his fingers through my hair, and gripped to pull my head to the side. He wanted to kiss and keep me connected to him in every way. He moved and my body was set ablaze. My cock swelled and ached as I rutted into the mattress with his thrusts.

"You're too hot, baby. I need to cum." His thrusts quickened. My balls clenched and wanted to pull into my body. My whole body quaked and my muscles tightened.

"Do it, please, I want your cum." I spilled onto the sheets and he growled in my ear as he came, pushing me deeper into the bedding. We heaved together and fell back down to earth. I wanted to touch him, but I couldn't move.

"Holy fuck…" He breathed deep at my hairline and his hands swam over my skin as he rolled off me. I felt a hollow space as he left me, but he turned me and tucked me into him. I was eviscerated and didn't know where to go from here.

Some time later I woke up. We were still in the same place, still covered in cum, but I was definitely missing some time. "Welcome back, baby. You fell asleep for a while. I must have worn you out."

"I fell asleep on you." I hid my face under his arm.

"Don't hide from me. I'm pretty proud of the fact that I tired out my dirty boy. You were wild. There were words and noises coming from you that I never thought I'd hear." I dug my face in deeper and mumbled into the mattress. "It was amazing, babe. You're sensation-al." I looked up at that.

"Really? I know I never—I felt... It was amazing, but it was for you too? I just mean, you have been with..."

He pressed a chaste kiss to my lips. "It was perfect. I have never felt *that* before. We were so good together. Now don't give any of those doubts a second thought. We should probably get you cleaned up."

"My bathroom is pretty tiny. I wouldn't get any ideas," I laughed. "Besides, I am exhausted. You did wear me out, old man." He leaned down and swatted my ass. "Hey! I was joking. Why don't I wash up and you can get in bed and get comfortable?" Caine reluctantly agreed, and I went to clean up. When I got back, Caine had stripped and remade the bed. I watched his naked body as he fluffed the pillows and crawled into my bed. I went over to the dresser, but Caine's voice stopped me.

"You're not about to put on pajamas? Uh uh, you wouldn't want me to feel uncomfortable because I'm all naked on my own, would you?" He fluttered his lashes, feigning innocence. I dropped my towel and attempted a sexy strut to the bed to join him. We teased and touched late into the night, talking till we fell asleep.

14

CAINE

I woke up on Saturday morning way too early for anyone sane. The sun was long from rising, but I could hear Hulk pawing at the bottom of the door to try to get into the room. Logan had rolled away from me in the night, but he trapped my arm under his elbow. I decided to let him keep it. I was pleased that the whole time I've been with Logan I have never questioned my feelings or been frightened off by the thought of committing to him. I wanted more with him. I wanted everything from him, but I knew he was worried I wouldn't want him for long, and I worried I'd hurt him if I moved too fast. I wanted to run with him because walking didn't feel right, but I didn't want to risk his heart. My lips found his shoulder blade and I scooted closer to hold him. I dozed off with him in my arms and woke up later to a pleasant surprise.

"Logan?" I watched his head pop up under the sheet, but he didn't say anything. I felt his teeth nip at the muscles in my abdomen. This was bold and very unexpected, but damn, he was good at it. I felt precum touch my groin, followed by Logan's tongue gliding along the hair at the base. "Mmmm..ugnngh–Lo–Logan..." He tugged at my balls and then his lips kissed the crown of my cock. He licked the slit then proceeded to take my dick in his throat. I couldn't help it. I thrust forward and made him gag. "Sorry–so–good..." Logan gripped the base of my shaft with his other hand and took me back in his mouth. I used all my limited faculties to try and stop squirming so I wouldn't choke him. He picked up speed and massaged my balls as he bobbed. I lifted the sheet so I could see this fucking sexy man devour my cock. His eyes were closed and his skin was flushed. He looked so eager and... "Fuck, I'm close. Please Logan––oh yea!..uhhhhhh." I lost it, and I felt him swallow as my dick twitched in his mouth.

He moved off my hips and scrambled over to the other side of the bed. I jumped on him, searching for his lips, and I tasted my cum as I swept my tongue against his. "That was a NICE way to wake up, baby. Can I return the favor?" I said in a lilting tone.

"N–no, that's okay. I'm fine." I watched as he tucked the sheet tightly around his top. I was confused. I know he's self conscious, but he just had my dick in his mouth and blew my mind–*pun intended*–and now he doesn't want an orgasm.

"You just gave the best morning bj, and now you don't want your own?"

"It's not that–I just..." He sighed, so crushed. My brain worked to read between the lines. And then it hit me. He closes his eyes during dancing and sex; he hides his face and body. He gave me a blowjob so I wouldn't try to touch him, or at least to try and distract me.

"This is about your stomach, isn't it? You're worried that I'll have to get up close and personal with it when I'm down there and what––it'll disgust me?" His eyes welled up with tears that didn't fall. "Oh baby, how could you think that?"

"It's just that my belly lays on my groin and you might have to move it to touch me." His face was so tortured as he waited for me to say something.

"So then I lift your belly. Baby, it's a part of you, and I think it's sexy. You're sexy, and just what I want." I could practically hear the silent 'for now' he was adding in his head. Compliments weren't working, because they went in one ear and he distorted them into whatever his mind told him to. I sat in front of him on the bed and gripped his shoulders. "I'm not asking you to change how you see yourself. I just need you to believe that I like what I see, I love what I see, because I see you." It all sort of slotted into place in my mind. I think I just said I love Logan. *So much for not rushing him.*

15

LOGAN

Did that just happen? No--really, that didn't. He didn't mean to imply that he loved me. Even if in that jumble of pretty soothing words, he meant that he loved me, did I love Caine? Do I believe he loves me? I mean, it's been a week. He must be crazy if he thinks he loves me. But I must be crazy too. What should I say? He didn't actually say the three words. All three were in there, but not, like, together. I can't ignore it and now it's been too long and it's getting weird....

"Logan, I love you, if that wasn't clear. I know I probably said it too soon, so you don't have to say it back, but just know that I've never said that to anyone before."

Silence

I don't know if I can say it. I want it. I want his love and I love him, but I don't know if I can actually make the words come out. I stare at him. He's not upset or about to laugh it off. He's just waiting–patiently. Waiting so long. I got out of bed and slowly walked to the bathroom and closed the door.

Turning on the water, I ran my hands under the flow and then patted my face. I couldn't see it. I couldn't believe it. I saw my face in the mirror and didn't get it. I looked down at my body and didn't get it. I called out to him, but couldn't bring myself to open the door. "Caine!" I heard him run to the door.

"Logan, are you alright?--Really, it's okay if you can't say it back now. I understand. I'm not going to leave you."

"I need you to," I said into the door. "I need little time to myself."

"So you want me to go?"

"Yes," I whimpered.

"Can I call you later to check in--please?"

"Yeah, If you want," I choked out. I heard the bedroom door open and close. I waited in the bathroom, hiding from everything, when all I wanted was to hide from myself, not Caine. Caine who did nothing wrong. Caine who says he loves me! And I just let him walk away. No, I told him to go. What the fuck is wrong with me?

I stayed in the bathroom for--a while. I'm not sure how long. Eventually I ventured out to the bedroom, needing to put on some clothes. I forced Hulk into a hug; she squeaked and jumped out of my arms. She is so weird, though, because she came right back for more love. A few minutes later, I heard the door open and a familiar voice.

"What the hell happened, Logan?" Syl came walking in and looked at me pityingly all wrapped up in the bedding that smelled like Caine alone with my cat. "Logan, I got the most bizarre call, from your phone, from Caine, saying that you needed me and to get here quick. What did he do?" His fury reached my ears and that's when I cried.

"He loves me! He loves me and I made him leave!" Bawling at this point, Hulk ran away and Syl came by my side to hug me.

"Tell me everything and we'll figure it out." So I did. I told him all of it, even the steamy bits. And he listened to me pour my heart out. "Let me get this straight, your man of one week surprises you with a Valentine's night full of your favorite things, survived a Hulk attack, gave you a bone melting orgasm, and then professed his love in a rather Bridget Jones moment and you ran him off?!? Tell me what he did. Did you argue or say the wrong thing?" he asks exasperatedly.

"There was no fight, there was no argument at all. I just lost it!"

"What were you thinking? Do you not love him?"

"Of course I do! I know it's so soon and we are both crazy, but yes! I love him! I just can't believe he loves me back. That he said it first. It just doesn't make sense."

"Logan! Take a deep breath and then come with me over to the mirror. That's it, now look." I didn't want to. I spent far too long looking and loathing myself all morning. But if I knew Syl--and I did--he was trying to make a point. "When you see yourself. What do you see?"

"Bulk and flab. If I have to be positive, my smile is nice, and my eyes look pretty when I'm having a meltdown."

"When I look at myself I see a skinny beanpole with gap teeth and acne scars, but you know what the difference is? I know that others don't notice that first, or maybe at all. Men flirt with me because they like the packaging. I might think I'm damaged goods some of the time, but that's because it's MY insecurity."

"You're beautiful, Syl."

"So are you, Logan."

I looked in the mirror again. I still didn't like what I saw, especially since I was all puffy and bleary. But I thought I understood where Syl was going. He has insecurities, but they're personal. Mine are personal too. It only holds me back as much as I let it. Easier said than done, I know, but even I know confidence is sexy. That's one of the reasons I love Caine, for his boundless confidence and for the bits of confidence he inspires in me. And I hurt him.

"He has to be so upset, Syl. He told me he loved me and I just shut down."

"Didn't seem upset to me, just worried––about you. I think we should get you some breakfast and then we should take you to talk to Caine. You have something important to tell him." Winking at me while giving me a nudge to get out of bed and head to the kitchen, we sat and talked about our Valentine's night. Syl's date did not end in true love, but it was okay. They decided not to see each other again. When I told him that Hulk landed on Caine as things were heating up between us, Syl just about died laughing. My head was clearing from its fog, but I still worried about how Caine would be when I saw him again. I was a real shit for just walking away from him when he was putting his heart on the line. I just hoped I could make it right.

16

CAINE

I left Logan's bedroom and got dressed in the living room. I wasn't sure exactly what was happening with Logan, but I knew I didn't want him to be alone for long. I had Syl's number from the afternoon we all hung out at the bar last weekend, so I pulled out my phone and called him as I made my way down the stairs. He screamed at me for a bit, asking if I hurt him and what I did, but I just let him go on. Eventually there was a break in his lecture, and I just said that he needed to come be with Logan. I felt like hell for hanging up after that, but I just needed to clear my head. I didn't blame Logan for anything. Clearly I made a mistake telling him I loved him so soon. I knew it would be, but it just slipped out, and then I just wanted him to know.

I drove off in the direction of the bar. I didn't feel like going home on my own and I knew Em would be there since he rarely left. I replayed the whole night in my mind over and over. It was so perfect, making Logan cuss and talk dirty just by driving him crazy with want, laughing on the couch as he checked me for cat scratches, and watching him doze off in my arms tired from making love. That's what it was. Sure, it was hot and sweaty, but sex never felt like that before. It was different because I wanted him, not just release. If I could only have a redo of the morning. If I had stayed awake, we could have just started the day with breakfast together, or maybe I would have given him the blowjob and he would have woken up so needy his insecurities would have left him.

I parked near the entrance and went inside in search of a drink and my friend. I walked through the back and up the stairs to Em's place and knocked. I knew it was still pretty early, and he had probably been up late closing up the bar. Emmett opened the door wearing just his sweatpants, and all I could think of was how precious Logan looked in his pajamas. I wanted to be back with him, and my distress was written all over my face.

"What the hell happened to you?" Emmett said, rubbing the last few moments of sleep from his eyes. I frowned. He squinted his eye and looked me over. "What's wrong? You have sex hair, but you don't look happy? Shouldn't you be with your boy being all romantic and shit?" I managed to frown even farther. "Come in, give me a minute to get a shirt and my glasses. You make some coffee." So I did, and I put a healthy shot of Jameson in mine.

Emmett came back to the kitchen looking much less rumpled and ready to face whatever I had to tell him. He sat next to me and I slid a mug of coffee towards him. He leaned over and sniffed mine, no doubt noticing the heavy stench of booze coming off of it. "I blew it." I finally said.

"How? Logan seemed over the moon with you last weekend, and you surprised him for Valentine's day, right?"

"I told him I loved him."

Shocked, Emmett said, "You did what?"

"I told him I loved him." And then Emmett heard the whole story.

"It's going to be fine, Caine. Your boy was probably just shocked. Heck, so was I."

"You didn't see him. The look on his face; it was like he thought we were doomed."

"You're being preposterous. He might be a little scared, and things definitely progressed quickly between you two, but he'll come around. You told him to take his time with it, and he will. You can text him this afternoon to see if you can call or meet."

"I just can't lose him." We drank our coffee and I wallowed.

A while later there was a knock at Emmett's door. It wasn't un-usual to have managers and staff pop upstairs to ask questions or get assistance, but it was a little early at ten o'clock; only Kelly and a few openers would be here. Emmett rose to get the door, and a few moments later I heard my sweet boy and bubbles filled my blood.

"Uh––hi, Emmett, the uh––the bartender let me in and said it would be okay to come up. I––I'm looking for Caine. She thought he was up here."

"I'm here!" I said, the excitement and nervousness competing in-side me.

"Hi."

"Hey."

"Well, I am just going to pretend to do something downstairs. You two should talk," Emmett said, incredibly uncomfortable as he edged past Logan to leave.

"Do you want some coffee?" I asked lamely, just trying to keep the conversation going. I couldn't sit still. I kept running my hands through my hair, and Logan shuffled back and forth on his feet with his hands in his pockets. We made one fine awkward pair.

"Uh no, I'm good. Syl got me some and made me breakfast. Thank you for that by the way. I was a total butt to you and you cared enough to look out for me."

"Of course I did. Do––care about you. Look I know I pushed you too fast..."

"No! No––Caine, none of this was your fault. You were wonderful. And as far as taking things too fast, I thought we made our own rules." He gave a wry smile.

"We do, but I am well aware we need to get to know each other more before we can make big declarations." I was glad he was feeling better. His smile was small, but it hit my heart. "If I would have just kept my mouth shut."

"Please don't think that. You said––what you said––when it was right for you. And as far as us not knowing each other, that's true, there's a lot of territory to explore, but you knew who I needed when I was freaking out. You gave me space and comfort in the most perfect way possible. I just got in my own way, and I hurt you, hurt us."

"I'm not sure I understand why you shut me out. I know it was a lot to take in, but I really wouldn't have pressured you to say it back to me."

"I know." He hung his head and bit his lip. "I just couldn't believe it."

"Believe what?"

"That I could be loved." He looked up at me dejectedly, but with a trace of hope. "But leave it to Syl to convince me I'm worth loving and that my hang ups are mine. I shouldn't have let my mind put words in your mouth. Am I making any sense?"

"I think so. You're saying that your mind isn't to be trusted and you'd rather believe what I and others who love you see when they look at you." I said bluntly.

"In a much more poignant nutshell, yes." His face crinkled in amusement. "Like I said, I need to get out of my own way."

"I can't stop all the mean things your head might say about you, but I can keep reminding you how amazing I think you are." He blushed and sighed but looked me right in the eye.

"That's why I love you too--I'm sorry it came so late." I leapt forward and wrapped Logan up in my arms. I showered him with kiss after kiss till finally I slowed and my tongue found his. We stayed locked together until I felt his erection press into my thigh. If we had sex in Emmett's place he'd never stop disinfecting. So reluctantly I pulled back and placed one more kiss between his brows.

"Can I take you home with me? What I wanna do we can't do here, and if you want I can take you to my studio across town to stay the weekend."

"Yes please, Syl dropped me off here, so I'm all yours."

"Good, you're mine then. No getting away now." I saw the heat in his eyes and he didn't look worried or scared, just very inviting. I needed to get him to my house so I could ravage him senseless. "Let's give Emmett his place back, and we can pick up some early brunch on the way." I was hungry in more ways than one.

As we walked through the bar I saw Kelly, Russ, and Emmett hanging out with what I hoped were virgin mimosas since all three of them were on the clock.

"You two kiss and make up?" Kelly said.

"You better not have made up on any of the surfaces in my home." Emmett said sternly. Then added, "I'm glad you worked things out."

Russ, who had yet to meet Logan, mentioned that the 'pretty Pink Squirrel guy' already left and wanted him to pass on a message-- "Stop being stupid and I hope you can't walk for a week. I'll feed the beast this weekend. Call me!"

Logan cleared his throat. "That sounds like Syl, message received. Thanks."

We stuck around to get the pleasantries out of the way and I made sure it was still good with Emmett if I was scarce this weekend. I didn't want to have to step foot in the door until Logan had to go to work Monday. Logan tilted his head towards the exit to signal we should get on the road, and then I walked him to my car. We rested our elbows on the middle console and held hands while I drove. I made a quick pit stop to run into a shop for some sandwiches and a few baked goods so nothing would get cold if we got--distracted once we got home.

I gave Logan a quick perusal of my studio. Everything was all in one room except the big bathroom around the corner. I didn't live too far from the bar, and that cost a pretty penny, but the only things I wanted were close proximity to work and a large walk in shower. The view wasn't much, but if I opened the windows on a windy day I could hear the ocean. I tossed the food bags on the counter and turned to see Logan taking off his socks and shoes, but he didn't stop there. His jacket slid down his arms and hit the floor, then he gripped the hem of his shirt and ripped it up over his head. He saw me watching him and he licked his lips. My dirty boy was back and trying to seduce me.

"Put on a show for me," I said as I went to sit down on the bed. His whole body was rosy pink, but he kept going. He was trying to believe, trying to see himself through my eyes, and I was going to bask in his body. Leaning back on my elbows, I watched as he unbuttoned his fly with a flourish of his wrists. I smiled and he lost his seductive manner by chuckling behind his hands. "It's okay baby, keep going, I'm loving it." His gaze returned to mine and he bent his knees and pulled off his pants as smooth as is possible for skinny jeans. My brows raised when I saw his dark purple boxer briefs with tiny green polka dots all over. He was full of surprises, my fiercely fragile man. I lowered my hand to palm my dick through my pants as it throbbed. That must have got Logan going, because he took a deep breath and then slipped his fingers in the band and tugged them down. Just as fast, he stood up, tall and proud, wearing nothing but some silver chains layered down his chest. This confidence, whether fake or felt, was enthralling. I gasped in awe and he stayed silent, walking over to stand between my legs. I raised my arms as he pulled my shirt tail up and over my head and tossed it to the side. Leaning down to kiss me softly he fumbled along my belt. My hand moved from my cock to guide his wrist to the buckle, and I leaned further away so I could watch. The buckle clanked as it hit the hardwood floor and he opened my pants. Logan reached into my underwear and took out my cock. The silver from his chains chilled my chest as we kissed. He stroked me and I fell back on the bed. Logan let my erection lay on my stomach while he tugged at my pants and underwear. I lifted my hips to help him and he finished undressing me. He crawled on the bed beside me and started to lose his nerve.

"I'm not sure what to do next. I know…I know what goes where, but how do you want me?" He was timid now, but eager.

"I want you on top."

"You want me to top you."

"Well I'd like that too, but I meant I want you to ride me. Crawl on top of me and sit on my cock."

"I'll crush you!" Logan said harshly.

"You won't hurt me, dirty boy, and I won't hurt you. Trust me, you aren't too heavy. There's nothing I'd like more than to watch you bouncing on my dick." He nodded and I watched him struggle with his mind for a moment. "Condoms and lube are in the nightstand. Get yourself ready." That brought him back to me, so he moved to open the nightstand. He handed me the condom and I rolled it on and slicked myself up for him while he fingered his ass in front of me. He didn't turn around for me to see, but I saw his face. He closed his eyes in an attempt to protect his modesty, but I heard his breaths and groans as he scissored his fingers inside himself.

He crawled over to my side and braced himself with his hands on my chest as he swung his leg over my hips. Facing me, his eyes seemed uncertain, and he hesitated to put his full weight down on my abdomen.

"It's okay, you've got me, and I can't really go anywhere, now can I?" He laughed and I loved it.

"I told you sex is fun. It's ok to fool around."

He sat on me. The tip of my cock touched his crease, eager to get inside. I ran my hands up his thighs, skimming lightly with my nails till I reached his hips. He leaned down and caressed my collar bone with his lips and tongue. The sensation gave me shivers as he licked up towards my jaw then dipped his tongue in my mouth. We made out while his fingers felt my chest, tweaking my nipples and pulling till he made me groan in his mouth. "Fuck baby, you're so good. That's it, grind your cock into me. Oh please don't st..."--but he did. He stopped. My world spinned and I wanted his hands on me again.

"I want you inside me. I need to move." So he used my arm to lift up and grab my cock at the base to angle it. He swiped the tip along his crease, back and forth across his pucker. To get it in right or to torture me, I wasn't sure. Finally, I felt his hole give, and he moved down slowly, taking me in inch by inch till he was seated all the way to the bottom. I gave him a moment to adjust, but I needed him to move. He felt so tight inside. His channel clenched as he situated himself so he could ride me. I couldn't take my eyes off his body. Logan was breathtaking. He had no hair along his chest or belly, but a small patch of blond curls at his groin. His uncut cock leaked precum on my stomach. He placed his hands on my shins so he could work my cock against his prostate. He rocked on my cock and moaned. His chains were sliding across his nipples as he moved. It was a beautiful sight. My hands smoothed along the soft skin of his stomach and up to his chest to twist my fingers in the chains.

"Caine––please! I need your hand on my cock please..."

He writhed on top of me and I stroked his dick till it pulsed with cum, spurting and landing on my body and dripping down my hand. "Fuck, shit, you're so hot, so..." my cock was squeezed as he shot, making it impossible for me to hold on any longer. I let loose with a loud groan, and Logan fell on my chest, pasting our bodies together with his cum. I grabbed the bottom of the condom and pulled out of him. Logan was panting from all the fucking hot work he just did, and the heat of his body on mine was so satisfying, like clothes fresh from the dryer. Logan stilled as he realized he put all his weight on me, then he gracelessly rolled off of me onto his side of the bed. He was wrecked, but his insecurity was sneaking into his expression. "It's okay baby. It's better than okay. That was the best sex I've ever had, and that says something considering how great last night was. I guess it's true what they say about make up sex." Logan gave a breathy laugh and tried to move the blond strands that had matted to his forehead with little success.

"What, that everything gets clammy and sort of sticky?" Logan said as he gave up trying to straighten his sex hair. He was adorable in a wet puppy sort of way, but he smelled like sex and citrus.

It always amazes me how cum and sweat can be the sexiest fluids in the world in the heat of the moment, but then the sex is done and suddenly you feel disgusting. Moving off the bed, I kissed Logan's shoulder and left to throw the condom in the trash and clean up a little. I came back with a washcloth and saw that Logan hadn't left the bed, but he had pulled the sheet up over his body. I walked to the bed, stood over him, and tugged the fabric to his knees. "I should clean you up a little. Then we can get cozy. I'm not ready for another round, but god, I wish I was."

"A brunch nap sounds good to me. You still haven't had anything today but coffee and booze."

"And you," I quipped and enjoyed Logan's shivers as I ran the washcloth over his skin. I sort of forgot the food. I sort of forgot everything––but Logan was looking out for me, or at least wanted to make sure I didn't crash so we could have sex again. I put the washcloth away and grabbed the food and tray to take to the bed. "I worked up quite an appetite with you," I joked.

"We're going to eat here?" he said, surprised.

"I don't want you leaving this bed till at least dinner. Besides, we should probably change the sheets at some point anyway. I'm not afraid of a few crumbs, are you?"

"Well––no, but I thought you don't seem like the breakfast in bed type. You seem like you like to get up and get started with your day."

"Well––" I mimicked Logan's tone, "This is brunch, and I am definitely up for that nap with you afterwards. My old bones are still used to staying up till three and sleeping in till eleven if I close the bar."

"This weekend really is a treat then. Our schedules don't really match up much, do they?" He furrowed his brow and grabbed a pastry from the tray.

"Honestly, this is probably the most time off I've had in a row in years. Emmett really does stay behind the scenes and I have never really minded letting the business dictate my schedule. Are you worried we won't see each other enough to make this work?"

"No, well, I'm more worried I won't have you as much as I want, but I know I can come see you at the bar sometimes when you work. I know my friends like hanging out there, and you look hot behind the bar, so that's a perk."

I laughed and so did he. The bubbles filled me and all felt right. We chewed and chatted till we had our fill and I caught Logan trying to hide a yawn. I put the trash and the tray on the floor and scooped up Logan to lay back in the pillows, only feeling a few crumbs scratch my skin. I rested my chin in the crook of Logan's shoulder and snuggled him close. I've never done this. I'm not a cuddler, but you couldn't pry Logan from my grasp right now. This delicious escape in the middle of the day felt so out of place, but so absolutely necessary. My oxymoron of a man was slowly changing every aspect of my life into intense relaxation and fiery sweetness. I loved it.

17

LOGAN

I woke up and I wasn't alone. Caine was wrapped around me with his legs intertwined with mine and his arm around my stomach. I needed to pee and probably shower, so I stealthily unraveled from Caine and tiptoed through his studio to his enormous bathroom. It was the size of my bedroom at home. My whole bathroom could have fit in his shower. I relieved myself and turned on the hot water. The steam filled my vision, and I quickly understood the appeal as I stepped into the rainhead shower. It felt phenomenal as the water streamed over me. Caine might need to be careful or I'd never want to leave --and the thought of shower sex was an actual tempting possibility and not a fumbly frustrating mess like it would have been in any other bathroom. There was even a shower bench on the side. I imagined bending over for Caine to take me right there and then briefly wondered how many other men he had bent over there--but that was his past and I was okay with it. If I looked as good as Caine, I'd probably have more notches on my belt too. I go back to thinking how nice shower sex could be while I finish cleaning up, but I don't touch myself, wanting to save my pleasure for him.

I heard Caine waking up as I got out of the shower. I imagined his back muscles shifting under his skin as he stretches and flexes to wake up. I liked spending the whole day with my boyfriend––I guess that's what we were now. I thought about it as I dried myself off, feeling unsure about what Caine would call us. Neither one of us has ever been in a relationship before. I listened as he grunted and grumbled on his way into the bathroom. He was still gloriously naked with his eyes only half open. He slid his hand up my neck to grip my damp cheek, and in a voice dripping with sincerity said, "You are beautiful." And he left it at that.

I beamed and my mind somersaulted. I didn't feel the urge to correct him or laugh it off. I just felt his love wash over me. Even when he's bleary eyed and blurred with sleep, he still thinks I'm beautiful––and I think he's indescribable. So with no words to tell him just how I feel about him, I stupidly say, "Are we boyfriends?" and then smack my hand to my forehead.

Caine turned and his mussed features crinkled cutely. "We're something. Boyfriends, sure, but that sounds a little more fitting for your twenty-five years and kinda icky with my thirty-five."

"You're not old. You're just older than me."

"Oh, I know I'm not old, not really. I just don't know if I like 'boyfriends.' It sounds too temporary. We'll think of something good, but if you meant to ask me if we're exclusive, then yes. No doubt."

"No doubt, really? I'm sorry, I don't mean to keep going back to this, but with all the guys you've been with, you're okay with only being with me?"

He chuckled and rubbed his eyes. "Wow, you must really think I'm a slut. Haha. You wouldn't have been wrong a week ago. I had sex with a lot of very attractive men, but I've only ever 'been' with you, and I prefer it."

"But I'm not attractive with abs and biceps and all..." I waved my hand to gesture up and down at the adonis in front of me.

"Just because you aren't attracted to yourself doesn't mean that others can't be. You might not be your type, but you are mine." Caine stepped towards me and held me to him, starting to kiss my neck and nibble at my ear. I wanted to get swept away by him, but my negativity still niggled at me.

"Sorry for dragging my insecurities into..." He put a finger to my lips and shushed me, then playfully bopped my nose with his index finger.

"No apologies. I need to hear when you feel these things no matter how down you get. I promised I'd build you back up, and while sex is magical, it's not going to fix everything. You need reassurance, and I love giving it to you in all ways."

"Damn, you're perfect," I said, because damn, he is. The moment called for a curse.

"I'm perfect for you and you're perfect for me." And he's right. I know these are new love butterflies and that we still need to learn and grow together, but I see that we can. This is not just lust or an infatuation; this is genuine love in its earliest stage. I bounced back to reality when I felt Caine grab my butt. "You have the most luscious ass I have ever felt," he continued as he nuzzled back into my neck. "My dirty boy is too clean. Mmm—why would you shower without me? Let me mess you up again before we wash."

And that's how I had shower sex for the first time. It was still as slippery and fumbly as I thought it would be. There were lots of laughs wriggling around trying to get situated, and I think I might have bruised my tailbone, but it was awesome! Seeing Caine's toned body all soapy and wet was quite literally like a porno come to life. We found our rhythm in the steam and started heating up. I was a little sore though. I was not used to have quite so much sex, let alone the earth shattering kind. He fondled my body till my cock ached. He groped me in all the places I feared and avoided, reveling in them with satisfied grunts and growls. He sucked and marked my skin with his lips and stubble. It was all too much; I was in exquisite pain waiting for him to touch my cock. Caine was as hard as stone and in as much need as I was when he grasped his own cock and then mine, rubbing us together in the most erotic masterbation I could ever imagine.

"Ah, fucking hell, you feel so good." Shoved up against the wall with my back feeling the smooth tile, hot water beating down as he beat us off, I couldn't deny how fucking good it felt.

"Fuck, Caine, don't stop. Yeah, uhhh yes, ehh." My balls rose up and I felt Caine's dick twitch against mine. "I want to cum. Please I wanna...."

"Cum baby; cum for me! Uhhgnnh." We spilled all over the shower floor. Sloshing over to sprawl along the shower bench, I was done––so done––like couldn't imagine ever being able to have sex again I was so worked over. However, realistically, I knew it was only early evening, and while dinner and cuddles were in my future, I didn't think we'd keep our hands to ourselves ALL night long. I just needed a break.

Once we mustered the strength to clean up again we got out of the shower and decided to go out for dinner. Caine ran me by my place to change and pack up a few things. Hulk was a little nicer to Caine, maybe trying to make amends for last night's sneak attack. She tried to mew at me to feed her, but Syl had texted that he stopped by earlier and gave her dinner. "You can't put one over on me. You're not getting extra food, you brat, and you better not throw a hissy fit." I stuck my tongue out at her and Caine laughed as she turned, flicked her tail, and strutted away.

"Aren't pets supposed to be fun and loving?" he asked.

"Oh she loves me, but it's only when she feels like it. Honestly, she can be downright cuddly and sweet in short bursts, and she sleeps with me every night. You've really never had a pet?"

"I think I had a fish when I was little, but I won it at the fair so it didn't last long. Other than that, no. With the hours I keep, it just wouldn't seem right leaving them home alone all the time."

"Well, you wouldn't know it by Hulk, but cats are pretty low maintenance. Sure, they like to be petted from time to time, and maybe they would curl up with you when you're home, but they like to chill and do their own thing. Actually, a lot of pets can be like that, except for maybe dogs. My family had one of those when I was little and they love attention and people."

"Should we take her with us?"

"What?" I asked, puzzled.

"Hulk, should she go with us back to my place? Or should we come back here later instead?"

"You're too much. She is important to me, so thank you, but I'm not sure you're ready for a cat box at your house when the cat isn't even yours."

"Eh, she's growing on me. Besides I want you at my house more too, so if that helps, then I'll make a spot for it and Hulk-proof my house."

She must have heard her name, because all of the sudden she was there rubbing her face against his pant leg--*such a suck up*. It endeared him to me even more. My cat has been nothing but trouble to--well, everyone but me, and he was willing to change his tidy studio to take in my little monster so I could be happier.

"Not this time, but maybe we can get a few cat things for your house for the future." The future, man, didn't that sound good. I could see it, still a little fuzzy from fear, but I wanted that future and actually believed it could happen.

We said goodbye to Hulk and went to dinner at a little seafood place by the beach with fantastic steamed shrimp; Old Bay should be put on everything. We went for a walk along the shore. It was chilly but beautiful watching the waves crash with nothing lighting our way but the moon and ferris wheel lights from the pier in the distance. While my shoes were much more comfortable this time, I did take them off to squidge the sand in my toes and feel the grit as I walked along holding Caine's hand. The evening was nice and mellow, or at least it was till Caine said, "You should come with me to lunch with my mother tomorrow," in the most casual tone, like he was saying 'I like tacos' or 'do you want fries with that,' not the bomb he just dropped of me meeting his family!

"Uh, maybe we should give it more time--you know. Springing a stranger on her at the last minute is a real party foul."

"She knows about you." My mouth gaped.

"She knows about me? How? When? We just became the equivalent to boyfriends this afternoon. When and why does she know about me?"

"I told her. Look, I don't date--so the fact that we had more than one date was newsworthy. Ma is really cool. You really don't need to worry. She'll love you like I do. Besides, she'll just be happy to talk about something other than the bar."

"I didn't prepare for this. I only brought random clothes to hang around with you in, not something meet-the-parents worthy. I don't want to embarrass you."

"Oh my god, stop. You look ridiculously good in everything, and I saw you pack some killer accessories she'll love. We're just going to lunch at Lacy's down the street from the bar for some pizza. You'll knock her socks off. This is a good thing. I want her to meet you."

"Okay, yeah, you're right. She sounds fun from what you've told me. It's a good thing. I just freaked for a minute. I'm honored to meet you mother."

"Good," Caine said, and we walked back to the car and brushed off our feet, hoping to not take too much sand back to his place. I'm anxious but excited to meet his mom. I don't have much experience with moms. Mine died when I was little, and Syl's whole family pulled away from him once he came out after high school. They always suspected, and Syl wasn't exactly subtle with his makeup and flair for all things tight and showy, so they had kept their distance. Apart from Syl, who Caine could never avoid, I didn't have family to introduce him to. Not blood anyway. Like I told him, my dad and I weren't close, not because I'm gay, but because we just never really had much in common and he just went through the motions of life after mom died. I don't think he cared that he had a son, and it has always been that way. It's just the way it is, and we haven't talked since I left my hometown six years ago. I made my family. It was Syl and Devon, and now his partner Samuel was a core member of our little group. Maybe Caine would want to meet them soon.

We drove back and had an epic necking session on Caine's couch, which slowly heated and turned more into canoodling before clothes started flying. Caine laid me back on the couch and I could tell where he was headed. He slid down so his knees hit the floor, and his face was incredibly close to my crotch. I focused on his hungry eyes instead of thinking about my paunch and how not sexy I was at that angle, but I didn't see any of that in his face, and I relaxed more as his lips met my inner thigh. Mmmm. I bit my lip and whined as his mouth reached my groin. In all the intimate ways he's touched me, this made me feel the most exposed, but it also felt marvelous. It was just kissing, but I squirmed and my cock would be screaming right now if it could.

"Come on Caine, please." He lifted his head to look at me, resting his chin right on my erection. *Sadistic bastard,* how did he do this to me? I never talked like this, never thought like this. I never talked at all during sex, and no one ever talked to me, just moans and groans till it was over.

"Please what, baby?" God, how could he use that innocent tone when he was doing what he was doing? It wasn't fair.

"Please suck me––please suck my––suck my cock."

"That's it. I want to hear you. I want to know how I make you feel. Give me noises, words, whatever you can." And he sucked me in, the whole way down to the base. Uuuh, I would tell him anything he wanted to hear, but I didn't know what to say. I didn't want to think of words, so I just made sounds, muffling them with the side of the couch cushion. He slowed down, lifting to the crown and then taking me back down. I felt his throat swallow around my cock, and I pulled my head out of the cushion to watch him. His dark eyes were wet, and he watched me watching him, treating me to a slow suctioned pop as his mouth slid off my cock. It was the sexiest thing I had ever seen until....

"Oh shit, yes!" I saw him twirl his tongue around my head and lick the slit. "Damn, shit Caine! It feels so fucking good." He smiled an unholy smile and moved his hand to squeeze my balls and then went back to bobbing. I couldn't take much more, and I wanted to cum so bad, but I wanted to warn him.

"Caine I can't– I'm gonna––I need to cum." He pushed down to the base and held there as I spilled in his throat. Caine pulled off me and licked along the way for any drops leaking down.

"You taste good, dirty boy," he said, smacking his lips for emphasis. "And when you watched me I just about lost my damn mind." Curious, I leaned over the edge of the couch and saw his spend on the floor. "I had to get myself off. You were all needy and moaning, watching me blow you. I couldn't resist."

"I would say you robbed me of my chance to reciprocate, but I'm too tired to be mad." I giggled and saw him look at me adoringly. I've never been looked at like that before. It was piercing but gentle in its sharpness. I wondered how much farther I could fall for him.

"I'm glad you aren't mad at me for making you cum. Haha–but I promise I'm up for it anytime you want to give it––within a reasonable amount of time after the last orgasm."

Clearly he had no idea I was having romantic notions in my head, but that was fine. There was plenty of time for sweetness, and I knew he enjoyed being flirtatious and fun in bed––or on the couch. It was getting late, and I sure didn't think there would be a fourth round today, but cozy cuddles in bed sounded nice. So I kissed his swollen lips, picked up my clothes and put them away to wash later, and went to lay in bed. Caine watched me walk naked around his apartment with a pleased smirk on his face. It was wonderful being the center of his attention. I never wanted to be the center of anything before, but he was different. Caine was becoming my world. He followed suit and climbed under the covers with me. I turned his back towards me and made him the little spoon.

"You're like my personal electric blanket," he said sweetly, lifting my hand up to kiss it then return it to his stomach.

"If I'm too warm..."

"No, I like it. Cuddles were never really part of the deal with sex before. It's nice--more than nice."

I hugged him and didn't let go until I heard him snoring.

18

CAINE

Waking up to sweet sleeping Logan is something I would never get tired of. His mouth was open a little and there might have been drool on the pillow, but he was so peaceful laying in the morning sun coming through my windows. I have never slept as good in my life as I did with him holding me. I woke up rested with no alarm, and all that I thought was how sad that this couldn't last forever. Soon there would be schedules to navigate and nights alone when we couldn't work it out. I knew we couldn't stay in this state of perfection. This was a crazy wonderful twenty-four hours that I would never regret. We had today till I had to drop Logan back at his place for work tomorrow, and that was fine. It was ridiculous to think we could spend every waking and sleeping moment together even if I wanted to. I fell hard and fast for Logan, but I needed to remember that neither of us were going anywhere, and didn't they say absence makes the heart grow fonder?

I let him sleep as I went to shower and then laid next to him while I texted with Emmett to check in and see what challenges the week ahead would bring. Scrolling through social media, I saved a few memes to send Logan this week that I thought would make him giggle, and then I texted Ma to confirm our lunch plans. She was ecstatic that Logan was coming. I told her how nervous he was and asked her not to be too aggressive in making him feel welcome. I knew there was nothing to worry about. She would smother him with attention and embarrassing stories about my childhood while he would feel incredibly awkward till he laughed and relaxed. It would be--interesting, but a good time.

Placing a kiss on his temple, I rubbed his shoulder and gently shook him awake. He groaned and complained a little, but I wanted him to have enough time to get ready and freak out, plus I had to factor in the sex we would have to distract him. "Wake up, love. We need to start our day."

"I don't wanna."

"Yes, you do." I moved closer and pressed my bulge into his back.

"Mmm, I want, but sleep." I snorted and then ran my hand down his belly to his erection. He did want, and I could guaran--damn--tee you I could make this more appealing than sleep. I ran my fingers feather light up his shaft and felt the goosebumps perk up on his skin. He rolled over on his back and looked at me with a big pout on his face. "You don't fight fair."

"And I never will," I said as I pressed my lips to his. "Will you fuck me baby? It's been a while, but I liked that idea the other night." That made him wide awake.

"I can--but I've never topped before," he said shamefully. I rolled my eyes.

"Fuck the men you've been with before. It's fine, baby. We'll start slow and I'll finger myself open for you. No worries." I grabbed the lube and passed him a condom. I turned to show him my ass. I didn't fool around preparing myself, but I made sure I would be comfortable taking his cock. I was worked up and ready, but when I was done he looked lost. Lost in me? Lost in what to do? I wasn't sure. "Do you want me on my back or front?"

"Back, on your back please." He was so shy. I hated making him uncomfortable, but I knew he'd love this once he got started. I laid down and spread my legs for him while he scooted closer. Logan bowed down to kiss me. I felt his hands roam my chest, cupping my pecs, rubbing my nipples with his thumbs. I held his face to mine. He looked so nervous and his lips quivered.

"You aren't going to hurt me. You aren't going to be bad at this. You're such a sexual being. You just have to let go. And if it's rubbish, practice makes perfect." I gave him another kiss and a wink. "I would happily practice with you over and over and..."

"I get it," he scoffed. "Just help me along a little and tell me if I need to move or something. Okay?"

I nodded and he sat back on his knees. Lifting my hips up, I angled my ass to rest on his thighs, and he grabbed my legs to place them on his shoulders. His cock pressed against my hole, and the pressure at my rim was profound. A bittersweet heat filled me as he eased in. I inhaled to relax, "God, baby, you feel amazing. More please--baby." Still slowly, he moved till his stomach touched the back of my thighs, and he folded me to push in more. Unable to wait, I flexed my hips and beared down on his cock. "Ahhh yes, oh god, please move. Fuck me."

"You feel--sooo-tight." He wrapped his arm around my legs and gripped my ass with his hand, cradling it as he leaned in to thrust.

His weight pressing down on me sank him in so deep. I didn't know what to do with my hands. I couldn't reach his body and I needed something before I imploded. I fisted the sheets in mouthwatering agony as he repositioned. Gaining confidence as he heard me moan, he picked up speed and planted his hands on my chest. I grabbed his wrists tight for hold so I could move my hips to meet his thrusts. "You're so fucking hard, Caine. Stroke yourself and cum for me."

"Dear sweet fuck, yes!" I grabbed my dick and followed his demands. He pounded into me. "So fucking hot--dirty--boy, huhh..." I bit my lips hard, and the pain was fucking unbelieveable mixed with Logan hitting my prostate with every beat. "Close, baby boy--fuck, so close!"

"Ugh hhhhhmm!" Logan screamed as he came and it sent me over the edge.

We laid there tangled, blissed out, and spent. I liked being fucked. It was a rare occurrence, but not anymore. "Damn, you're good at that--and so commanding."

"That was so good. Caine, your lip is bleeding!"

"Oh, it's fine; that felt good too. Turns out I might like a little pain with my pleasure." I waggled my eyebrows at him as I licked my lips. "What? I might have to start calling you sir. I quite like the sound of that actually." I smiled and he scoffed.

"No thank you. I am not running this show. You be sir."

"I like the sound of that too." I gave him a peck on the lips. "But you have to do all the sexy things I tell you to then."

"That might not be too bad. You haven't steered me wrong yet."

"How do you feel about spanking?" I joked, although who knows where we'd go down the line. I might like it. Logan has a little spice in there and I think it matches mine.

"Hah I--I don't even know if you're serious, but--maybe." He shrugged and giggled. I liked this frisky side of Logan. It's a shame it would disappear as soon as I reminded him that we needed to get ready to meet my mother. I sat up to break the news.

"Hey sweetheart, I..." He stopped me and straddled my lap. "Um, as sexy as this is, there's no way I'm up for more. Besides--" He stopped me again.

"I need your help." I looked at him, clueless as to what he could want. "You call me baby, sweetheart, and things in bed, like--dirty boy." Logan whispered like it was a secret. "But I don't know what to call you. Nothing's fit and sir is still up in the air. You need something else."

"You can call me anything you want. How about snookums?" He shook his head forcefully. "Sugar lips, snugglepuss, super stud..." Logan was so not having it. "I know, I've got it, Big Papa!" He actually slapped my shoulder at that one. "Really babe, I just call you what rolls off the tongue. When I first saw you I called you bubbles in my mind."

"Bubbles? Why?"

Your laugh was infectious, effervescent if you will, and I felt my blood simmer, and my body fills with bubbles when you laugh or make me happy. It's just what I thought. Bubble boy in the streets, dirty boy in the sheets."

"Oh my gosh, you're ridiculous." He kissed me and gazed into my eyes. "Hero," he said. "I'll call you--hero. That's how I see you."

"Well--shit, bubbles, I go and say something absolutely over the top and you get all seriously romantic on me." Wow-just-- wow, my face heated and I looked away from him. I didn't know what to say. I didn't want to joke more. I tried, but I couldn't laugh at that. He's too good for me and he's oblivious to all my flaws and all his greatness.

"You know I'm not perfect, right? I'm no hero. I'm going to fuck this up at some point. I just want you to know I'll always bend over backwards to fix it. I don't want to lose you."

Alarmed, he said, "Whoa, hey–– I'm not going anywhere. I don't think you could get rid of me. Why would you lose me?"

My eyes welled. I was fucking crying. He's so damn wonderful he broke me with his sweetness. "Look, Logan, I know you think I'm great, but I just look good. In reality, I cuss worse than a sailor, work almost twenty-four seven, and I have no clue how to be in a relationship." Oh fuck, now I'm going to make him cry. He wiped the tears from my eyes and took in a few deep breaths.

"Caine, I don't expect perfection, and I don't need you to always have an answer. I'm just as unsure as you, but you make me feel good and feel good about myself. You're a good man and what I need to save myself. You keep me grounded and flying through the clouds at the same time. That's why you're my hero. That's what made me think of it. Well, that and an obsession with men in tights."

"Damn bubbles, what are you doing to me?" We laughed and my random emotional outburst was quelled. We kissed and when we parted I saw the time. I couldn't leave it any longer. "Hey sweetheart, I'm not sure if you remember, but we need to meet my mom in like two hours."

"What?!?" He scrambled off me and looked at the clock. "You let me do that to you right before we meet your mother! Oh good grief, how am I going to face her when I have fresh images of you like that in my head?"

––And my dirty boy was gone and wholesome Logan was back. "Don't worry, babe, it's okay. We'll save time and shower together," I teased and he glared. "And absolutely no funny business, cross my heart."

We scurried to get ready; well, he scurried. I stopped rushing after the shower. I threw on a royal blue polo and some jeans and called it a day. That was pretty dressy for a lunch at Lacy's. I let Logan be frantic, knowing my mom was at home searching for what to wear too. They had some similarities that I didn't want to dwell on because I like sex with Logan, but that's why I thought they'd get along.

When he started fretting and looking through his bag for alternative outfits, I stepped in. "You look spectacular." And he did look great. He had the bright pink shirt on he said Syl picked out for him at the mall, a gray moto jacket, and of course his tight ass dark skinny jeans paired with tiny pearl studs in his ears.

"I love you." He said, placing his hand on the back of my neck and pulling me down for a couple kisses.

" I love you too––and so will my mom."

I grabbed my coat, and Logan and I left to go to the restaurant, but he stopped on the way to pick up some flowers for my mom. I told him it wasn't necessary, but I knew it made him feel better not to show up empty handed, and my mom would think it was sweet of him. Surprisingly he seemed to relax the closer we got to Lacy's, and when we saw my mom waiting outside, he was calm and collected. She stood waving at us like we were a plane and she was stranded on a desert island. She practically jumped up and down as we approached. Mom pulled me in for a huge bear hug that stole the breath from my lungs and then moved to do the same to Logan.

"Alright Mom, I like Logan alive. Let him breathe." She let him go and threw her love back at me.

"Macushla, I'm so glad you aren't alone anymore!" She let go of me and grabbed Logan's shoulders. "And look at him; he's precious."

"Logan, this is my overly affectionate mother, Cathleen. Ma I told you not to come on so strong. At least buy him dinner first."

"Oh please Caine. Logan, it's wonderful to meet you, and none of this Cathleen business. I am Cathy or Ma. Are these for me? They are beautiful. Did Caine tell you that lillies are my favorite?"

This was going downhill fast. Logan was like a scared rabbit waiting to get eaten by a wolf, and my mom was still going, not even stopping for breath. Then Logan popped up with, "Macushla?"––and I was so happy he spoke up and got her to slow down.

"It's Irish Gaelic for 'darling;' she's called me that and many other Irish phrases throughout my life, many containing swear words. She really only ever uses Gaelic when she's mad at me or calling me darling. I get the cursing gene from her." This made us all laugh and then my stomach growled. "Let's go inside and get a table. We never ate breakfast. I'm starving."

"Oh, why didn't you two eat this morning?" It was then I knew I made a mistake. Logan's eyes went wide and he kicked me lightly in the shin. Ma pursed her lips and she followed up with, "Oh, okay––well you two must have worked up an appetite."

Logan snorted, knowing I had made almost the same joke yesterday. This was great, going just peachy. It could only get better and more embarrassing. Logan better get used to it, because I certainly am.

19

LOGAN

Oh my god, Cathy was crazy. She was hilarious and ferocious with love for her 'macushla.' *Swoon, so cute*--and she was absolutely gorgeous with Caine's dark auburn hair, a purple turtleneck, and some stunning filigree silver hoops. She had a lot more freckles than he did, or at least more on her face. Caine's were all over his shoulders and arms, mostly. Apart from that freakishly coincidental joke earlier, though, their personalities were very different. Cathy was pretty conservative, apart from her acceptance of her gay son and his sex life. I saw little hints of spicy here and there that mirrored Caine, but she was modest and matter of fact, neither of which she bequeathed to her son. But she was full of love and she took care of those around her --and that was Caine. I felt pretty comfortable as we talked and ate pizza together.

"So you two haven't been dating long, but you seem pretty close. Logan dear, what did you do to catch my boy? You must be pretty special to stop him from his philandering ways."

"Ma!" Caine scolded her, but I thought it was great. He was a self proclaimed slut after all. She just had a––slightly more polite way to put it.

"I'm not sure exactly what I did, but I do love you son. He makes me feel special, and I haven't had a lot of that in my life apart from my friends." Man, I know how to suck all the fun out of the room. I mentally facepalmed and quickly turned the conversation to tell her about Syl and how Caine and I got talking over his retro taste in drinks.

"Well, I'll have to try a Pink Squirrel sometime, sounds lovely. Macushla, it's been quite a while since I visited you at work."

I balked, "You went to––Built Bar to visit Caine?" As incredibly informed as she is, Cathy didn't seem like the kind of lady to go to any sort of club.

"Ma came when Emmett and I first opened up and sometimes visits before we are open to the public. Make no mistake though, Logan, she can cut a rug with the best of them."

"I've got moves. I just don't feel like gyrating and humping on the dance floor. You millennials can enjoy that all you want, but it's not for me."

"You're welcome for a drink or a dance anytime, Ma." Caine said, tenderness in his words. She reached over and patted his hand. The relationship they shared was unique, but I guess everyone feels that way about the people in their lives, whether the bond was strong or weak. The two of them seemed like they had been through hell and back together, but they focused on the good times they'd had. I enjoyed the way they bounced back and forth and finished each other's stories. It was nice to know that in time I would know the stories and Caine and I would have our own to add. I stopped my wandering mind and focused back in on their conversation.

"Oh, how is Emmett? Any changes in his health? Has he met some-one special too? It's been so long since I've seen him. Logan, those two are thick as thieves."

"He's Emmett, Ma, you know. He struggles and deals in his own way. He is doing more in the bar rather than just on top of it. We are planning an expansion for the future. Business is really good, and he knows he'll have to step up."

"You two work yourselves to the bone. How can you expect to have any time for love or friends or mothers when you add even more onto your plate?"

"I will always have time for you. And I will make time for Logan."

That brought fuzzy feelings to my heart and brought on an in-volved conversation about my job. I felt like I was an astronaut or something cool with all the interest she showed and not the pencil pushing number nerd I was. I enjoyed what I did, though, so I was happy to talk about it and listen as she told me about her years as a nurse. We talked for a few hours and ate till we were stuffed. We all left a big tip for taking up our server's table for so long, and then it was time for more hugs and goodbyes. I was given an open invitation to join Caine and Cathy anytime, and she even gave me her number so we could make our own plans. It was kind of surreal.

"I really like your mom. She's pretty amazing," I told Caine on the drive back to my place. We both agreed that I would go back home after so I could spend quality cat time with Hulk and get ready for the week. I was a little down about it, but Caine and I would call and text throughout the week and we made plans for next weekend. My friends and I were going to go to the bar. Caine would have a table for us reserved in case it got busy and he would join us when he could. He said Kelly would help him out and he would try to convince Emmett to cover him for a while too.

He dropped me off at my apartment building after lots of uncomfortable car kissing. I'm not exactly sure if that was the gearshift I felt, but if Caine was as hard as me I may never know. I offered for him to come up, but he claimed he wanted to remain a gentleman and if he came up he would have to remove my clothes with his teeth. I for one had absolutely no objections––but I saw his point that if he came up he'd never leave––again, NO objections here––yet here I am alone once again with a kitten yowling at me because I left her. *She's so dramatic.* I turned on the tv, made some pasta, and fed Hulk so she would settle. I got comfy with a fluffy blanket on the couch and Hulk curled up on my lap. I texted Caine to see what he was up to.

Logan: Long time no see ;) How's your night?

Caine: Better if you were here. Dic pic?

jk

Logan: Lol you're a menace

Caine: You say the sweetest things to me

Logan: Thank you for an amazing weekend <3

Caine: Best weekend of my life

At least till the next one

Logan: I love you Big Papa

lol

Caine: Oh yeah tell me more ;)

I love you too. Sweet dreams bubbles

Logan: Xoxoxo

It was nice to have a goodnight message, and I knew I'd have a morning message to look forward to. I snapped a cute picture of Hulk rolling over on her back for me to rub her belly to send to Caine tomorrow. She and I did this dangerous dance regularly. Hulk would expose her tummy for me to rub and then we both waited till she got sick of it and tried to bite me. I had a fifty fifty shot of her drawing blood or me being agile enough to pull my hand back; it was like a really funky version of chicken. Pet, pet, rub, pause–pet, pet, rub, pause–ah ha! I am victorious! *Hmmm, maybe Syl was right.* Well, I guess when you start declaring war on your cat, it's time for bed.

My bed looked so empty. I knew Hulk would join me eventually, but it just wasn't the same as having a strapping stud to curl up to. I tossed and turned, trying to find a comfortable position, but eventually settled into a deep sleep a few hours later.

20

CAINE

I missed Logan like mad. Sure, we talked and texted. Hell, we even had a couple steamy phone sex sessions; masturbation never felt so good––but I just wanted more. I wanted to see him and feel him. I knew if I asked, Logan would meet me for a quick bite or even stay over, but I didn't want to distract him from work, especially since he was up for a promotion if he did well with his current projects. Plus I had a ton happening at Built, playing catch up after being off. Don't get me wrong, Emmett could totally run this place without me, but we were still short staffed and there were just some things that get overlooked when you weren't out there everyday. We were missing a case of whiskey and our receipts weren't matching the amount of liquor used. That meant monitoring for over pouring or bartenders giving out too many drinks. Comping alcohol was fairly normal to make up for drinks made incorrectly or to make up for long wait times, and I didn't mind if my staff wanted to give a friend a drink occasionally, but this was way more than a couple free shots.

Somehow I made it all the way to Wednesday morning. God, I was a goner, doomed to be a lovesick fool, and I didn't even care. At lunch time I sent Logan a duck pic. Yes that's right –– a DUCK pic. A damn picture of a duck because I thought it was funny, okay? Apparently my boy thinks lame-ass things are funny too, because he called me on his break laughing so hard he cried. It might have had something to do with me sending one ––or two––mildly teasing texts before said duck pic. I think I underestimated how stupidly funny Logan would think the whole set up was, because he told me he almost got in trouble for hyena laughing at his desk––but I for one think I taught him a valuable lesson to not be on his cellphone at work. Oh, who am I kidding, I'd look at anything from him as soon as it came in. I was sort of getting desperate. The last text I sent him was at two o'clock, and I told him I missed him, but I didn't get a response. I hoped he wasn't upset about the duck or that he didn't actually get in trouble. I decided If I didn't get a goodnight text or call I would go to his place so we could kiss and make up. If I fucked up I'd own it. I was so relieved when I got the best surprise around six o'clock. Logan stopped by the bar after work to bring me dinner.

"Dumplings for my dumpling," he joked. "I would have brought duck, but I thought that would be in poor taste."

"Considering duck was a euphemism for cock and it would be torched, I really would have thought you were mad at me."

"I think a rooster would be the euphemism for cock; a duck would be dick. Why would I be mad at you? It was hilarious. Has anyone ever told you that you have great comedic timing?"

"Can you stay long?" I know I changed topics, but I just wondered how much time we had. The bar wasn't too busy right now, so I was hoping we could eat together.

"I was just going to drop it off and head home––but if you're saying you have a little time free, I could stick around a bit. What did you have in mind? A drink or…"

"Follow me," I said as I pulled him to the back office. I closed the door and pinned him up against it, forcing kiss after kiss on his willing mouth. I knew I couldn't fuck him at work, but I sure as hell wasn't going to let him leave without getting my fix. Only far too soon he came to his senses.

"Whoa there, tiger. I'd like to leave here without doing the walk of shame. What if one of your employees came back here?"

"I promise, all clothes are staying on. I just needed to taste you."

"You got your appetizer; now eat your meal," and he thrust the takeout in my face. "Besides, haven't you learned you shouldn't play with your food?"

"Ugh fine. I'll even open the door. Will you have dinner with me now?"

"Sure, but I don't want to keep you."

"They'll get me if they need me, and I've got to eat."

Our dinner was quick, and too soon we had to part ways. I gave him a chaste kiss and he left for home. I got back to work with only a little razzing from my bartenders. The night progressed fairly uneventfully. I had a few guys hit on me, but nothing more than innocent flirtation. I was off the market now and had no interest in anyone else. Sure, the guys were still attractive, but I was different. None of them even held a candle to the way I felt about Logan. When I look at Logan I see love. I feel his laughter. His charm lights up my life. I wouldn't dare risk all I had with him. He was special and he was mine.

21

LOGAN

Finally, Friday came and I was buzzing with excitement. Not only would I get to see my man, but Syl and I were meeting Devon and Samuel at Built around eight o'clock. Those two had a solid relationship like they were made for each other. They managed to live together and both work from home without wanting to kill one another. The two of them were inseparable. I thought Caine and I were similar––apart from the shared office space. He was always on my mind. I heard his voice when I got ready that morning telling me I was beautiful, and his sense of humor was palpable throughout my day. I was thinking thoughts I thought he'd think, if that makes any sense at all. I'm not even sure anymore because I was drunk on my handsome barman.

Syl came to my place to get ready and hang out until it was time to go. We had a bite to eat and I filled him in on everything that happened between Caine and I. Then I put on a little fashion show, impressing him by showing some pieces of color I added to my wardrobe this week.

"I think I really like this guy for you. If he finally gets it into your thick head how wonderful you are, then he has the Syl seal of approval."

"Say that ten times fast," I challenged him.

"Nah, I'm good. But really, hun, love suits you. Or maybe it's just the sex that's making you glow."

"Syl! I haven't even seen Caine since Wednesday, and we haven't been together since the weekend. Get your mind out of the gutter."

"So that's just happiness and spunk bringing color to your cheeks then."

"Syl!"

"Relax! Spunk is another word for confidence and you strutting your stuff. Now whose mind is in the gutter?"

"With as many jokes as you make about cum, I think you can understand why. You did that on purpose." I turned and saw the biggest grin on his face.

"Maybe," he shrugged. "Are you ready to go? Sammy just texted and said Caine sat them at the table."

"Samuel hates it when you call him that and yeah I'm ready now. I really hope they like him."

"Sammy loves it, and of all the things Devon calls him, this is tame in comparison. And Logan, if we see he makes you happy, then we'll all love him."

When we got to the bar, Caine was at the table with the guys. He looked so good tonight. He was in his classic fitted black tee and jeans, but there was something about it that just did things to me. Maybe because that's how I usually imagined himwhen I wasn't picturing him naked. He placed a peck on my cheek and stood up to pull out my chair. "Gin and tonic and a Pink Squirrel coming up," Caine said as he walked over to the bar to make the drinks.

"Is he always such a gentleman?" Samuel asked me.

"No–not–always." I gave him a wicked look and everyone laughed. "He is pretty incredible and thoughtful though," I added on, so they would know there was more than just the physical between us.

"He's in luuuvah," Syl said singsongy like a little kid.

"Syl, cut it out, but he's not wrong. We are in love. It just happened––well, after a tiny freakout."

"I helped him come to his senses and saved the day," Syl said smugly.

"You kinda did," I had to admit it.

Caine brought us our drinks, and we spent time talking all about first date stories. It was so nice to hear from Samuel and Devon. I know I shouldn't compare our relationship to theirs, and I wasn't really. It was just nice to know we weren't crazy for feeling an almost instant connection to one another. Syl cracked us up with some of his dating horror stories, and Samuel chimed in with some as well. Devon and Caine shared a penchant for fooling around prior to finding their boyfriend––or whatever.

Sadly, our boys' night was interrupted because Caine was called to help with the bar. I went back and forth getting drinks––and sometimes just going up to sit at the bar and ogle Caine. It worked out pretty well, and everyone was having a good time until a handsome man walked up to the bar. Caine stopped talking to me to take his order, which was just fine, but then the trouble started.

"I'll take whatever cider you have on draft, cutie."

"Coming up in one minute."

"What time do you get off work?" Handsome asked, and I winced a little when I heard that. I knew it was harmless and I trusted Caine. He'd just give the guy his drink, and then Handsome would just leave to dance or flirt with some other cutie that was available, because this cutie was mine.

"Really late, and I'm taken, sorry." Caine looked at me warmly.

"Oh come on, babe, we could have a real good time."

"I'm flattered, but no, I'm good." And Handsome did not like that at all.

"Can I get your number for another time?"

"I thought it was obvious, but..." Caine went and held my hand.

"You fucked him? Oh babe, you could do so much better than that fa..."

--And that's when I snapped. "Are you serious? He is mine and he's not interested in you when he has me." I'm not sure where it came from exactly, but I found myself standing up and getting really possessive.

Before I could get more riled up, Caine said, "My partner is right and I need you to leave. If you finish that sentence I'll have you escorted out."

He just said partner and we totally kicked ass together. Well, not literally, because I wouldn't want to hurt Caine's business, but the pissed off look on Handsome Shithead's face was great. It wasn't a big deal that Caine got hit on; that probably happened every night, but it was a big deal that I wanted to defend myself and not just accept what he was saying or jump into thinking Caine was better off with someone more attractive.

Caine took me from my thoughts and pulled me to the back. "I'm so sorry that happened, baby. I didn't want my past to interfere with us. I know I told you I hooked up with guys, but it's different when you see them come onto me, let alone outright insult you."

"I'm okay, Caine. I'm better than okay, actually. I trust you."

"But the things that dick said..."

"No, he didn't say it, because I stopped him and then my partner tossed him on his ass. It was kinda hot."

I walked over and planted a kiss on Caine's lips. He kissed me back, and it was possessive and fierce. He was mine and I was his. Now considering our friends and a literal bar full of people were waiting on us to come back, we couldn't get carried away. We'd save that for later tonight at my place.

22

CAINE

I closed up the bar and we drove to Logan's. Once inside, we picked up where we left off in the office. I kissed him the whole way down the hall and we closed the door so we could get some privacy from Hulk. Logan was insatiable. His hands went to undo my pants as soon as we neared the bed. There was no hesitation or caution in his movements. He pulled my cock out and started stroking me.

"Fuck baby––get undressed. I need you so bad." Everything was passion and fury as we moved. Clothes were off and his hands were on me again. I grabbed the lube and he rolled the condom down my dick. I sat on the bed back against the headboard and he straddled me. Moaning, he fingered his hole while my lips sucked and marked his body as mine. It was a whirlwind of sensations and sounds. He raked his nails down my back. "Shit––yes, baby. I want inside you." Logan grabbed my cock and placed it at his entrance. Too quickly I was inside him, and he sat down on my groin and began to rock.

"Ahhhh, fuck Caine!" He bit down on my shoulder to dull the burn. I hoisted him higher on my hips and squeezed his ass so I could fuck up into him. His hard cock rubbed along my abdomen, leaking precum. "Grab my cock. I need you--uhhh."

"Please Logan, cum for me. Fuck me hard and cum." I moved a hand to stroke him and he continued to ride me. I was so close, and I felt the pressure build as his channel tightened around me. I rolled my thumb along his crown and felt his cum shoot out in ropes between our bodies. He let out a heavy sigh of relief and I released inside him. Holding each other and panting to catch our breath, we slowly swayed back and forth, feeling the aftershock of our fuck. I rested my head on his shoulder and pulled him closer. This was wild and reckless, but even though it wasn't soft and gentle, it was love. I felt it mixed with heat, and as the fire fizzled, the love burned brighter.

We fell into bed and stared at each other, slightly stunned but deliriously happy. I liked this new side of Logan, all bold and possessive. I'd seen glimpses, but this was the first time I think he realized his power too. I loved him so endlessly, and I didn't want to imagine a future without him. Logan placed his hand on my cheek and pulled me in for soft kisses. His eyes held mine, and I knew we would face the world together.

23

LOGAN

I'm not exactly sure who that was just then, but I think it was me? The lust that was fueling me was probably ninety-nine percent responsible for the sexy beast that debauched Caine moments ago, but that other percent was--all me. It felt good. I felt good. Tonight I believed every bit of flattery Caine, Syl, and all my friends had shoved down my throat over the years. My body had not changed, but I think my mind had-- or maybe is starting to. I could just blame it on how love fixes all or that Caine has opened my eyes to the beauty inside, but that all sounds like lovey dovey phooey. I know I am pretty smart and hilariously funny, if I do say so myself, but something clicked, and I feel some of that positivity seeping in, like the rain fell down and washed away all the nastiness I saw before. I know I'm fat, but that doesn't seem to be such a bad thing anymore. I'm husky and hunky. I'm plush and pretty. I'm big and beautiful--and because **I** think it, it matters even more.

I am aware this is no miraculous thing. It is something that I'll have to work at, to practice, to flex my flaunt-it muscle, so to speak, but it's there, and I'm not faking it or pretending for Syl or anyone else. I actually feel it. It's me. This seed of confidence has been planted and is taking root, and I will get the cute gloves and a white watering can and whatever spades or tools I need to grow this puppy into a full fledged garden. It feels far too intoxicating to slip backwards. I was proud to be Caine's man tonight, and I won't feel bad for not being what that shithead expected. I am what Caine wants, and I want him and that's all that matters. I love this man. He is like a dream come true, and while he feels too good, I know he loves me too. I know I don't need to feel insecure about his affection and his attention all on me. I don't need to become what he needs, because I already am what he needs. I need him to.

We laid there in bed together watching, touching, and waiting for sleep to take us, too tired to care about cleaning up or even talking. He means the world to me. In such a short time, he has shown me so much, become so much. His natural caring nature, humor, and heat help me thrive. I know we can weather whatever comes our way. He'll look at me like he is now and he'll give me his strength, but that's for the future––our future–– and I can't wait to start.

Epilogue

Emmett – Three Months Later

Caine was driving me nuts. He and Logan found a new place together right down the street from the bar, which meant they lived right down the street from me. I was happy for them, really I was, but did I have to see the smitten looks on their faces all the time? I'm jealous, I know, but it's just hard seeing everyone around you moving on with their lives when you're still stuck in a cage of your own making.

My life changed five years ago, and now nothing was easy. I was in pain, and when the pain wasn't there, I was exhausted from not sleeping because of the pain. I craved order and some sort of control in my asymmetrical world. I worked and I hid, but now my work and my busybody friend wouldn't let me. I was trying. I covered for Caine so he could make goo goo eyes at his man, didn't I? Do I sound as bitter as I feel? I don't want to be. I can be a grumpy asshole when I hurt––and sometimes just because.

I like love. It looks sickening, but there's a real appeal. Can't I just be left alone, but not lonely? I used to run everything and felt on top of the world. Now I'm just lucky if I work up the nerve to leave my apartment without puking or sweating through my shirt. Most days I just don't leave if I can help it.

And now I've been putting these interviews off for as long as I could, but I knew we'd just get busier with summer approaching. Every time I did leave my apartment, I'd get hounded about hiring. I knew they were right, but I promised Caine I'd help him with the interviews, and let's just say my face doesn't always make first impressions easy. But I had to do this, to 'take small steps,' and so my staff wouldn't strike. I had to meet new people and ask them why they'd want to work for a freak.

A story doesn't need a villain when you are your own worst enemy.

Also By

About the Author

T.H. Compton is an avid reader and writer. The books she writes are the ones she wants to read, featuring characters she wishes were real, such as Syl from the Built for You series. In her opinion, books can provide a beautiful escape and lasting comfort if the characters strike a chord with the reader. If her books don't happen to be your Pink Squirrel, she hopes you can find your getaway from life with another author's words.

Love is for ALL

Support her on Patreon and receive sneak peeks and exclusives. Merch and books available on authorthcompton.com. You can go there to sign up for her newsletter so you'll never miss out. Want more pink squirrels and interaction? Join TH Compton's Pink Squirrel Squad on Facebook and be a part of her reader community.